AN ADAM WELDON

CYCLOPS
CONSPIRACY

WILLIAM
MᶜGINNIS

Whitewater Press
El Sobrante, California

Cyclops Conspiracy: An Adam Weldon Thriller
is available in print, ebook, and audiobook from your favorite retailer.

Published by Whitewater Press

Copyright © 2021 William McGinnis
www.WilliamMcGinnis.com

bill@whitewatervoyages.com
(510) 409-9300
5205 San Pablo Dam Road
El Sobrante, CA 94903-3309

Printed in the United States of America
First Edition: January 2021

10 9 8 7 6 5 4 3 2 1

McGinnis, William
Cyclops Conspiracy: An Adam Weldon Thriller

ISBN: 978-1-7336547-4-6

Cover design: Joseph Belocura Lloa
Book design by Andrew Benzie: www.andrewbenziebooks.com
Technical Assistance: Will Farley McGinnis

To Western Civilization.

CONTENTS

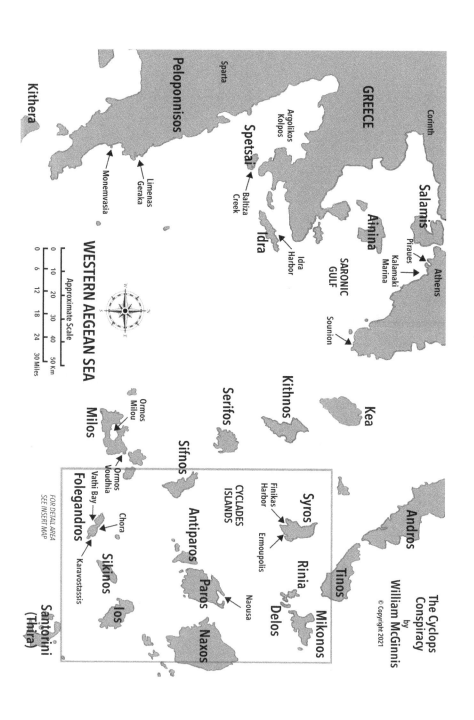

The Cyclops Conspiracy
by
William McGinnis
© Copyright 2021

WESTERN AEGEAN SEA

Approximate Scale

| 0 | 10 | 20 | 30 | 40 | 50 Km |
| 0 | 6 | 12 | 18 | 24 | 30 Miles |

GREECE

Corinth
Sparta
Peloponnisos
Monemvasia
Limenas Geraka
Kithera
Argolikos Kolpos
Spetsai
Baltiza Creek
Idra
Idra Harbor
Salamis
Piraues
Kalamaki Marina
Athens
Ainina
SARONIC GULF
Sounion

Kea
Kithnos
Serifos
Sifnos
Ormos Miliou
Milos
Ormos Voudhia
Vathi Bay
Folegandros
Chora
Karavostassis
Sikinos
Ios
Santorini (Thira)

Andros
Tinos
Syros
Finikas Harbor
Ermoupolis
CYCLADES ISLANDS
Antiparos
Paros
Naoussa
Naxos
Rinia
Delos
Mikonos

FOR DETAIL AREA
SEE INSERT MAP

Mikonos

Syros

Rinia

Delos

Finikas
Harbor

Ermoupolis

Naousa

CYCLADES
ISLANDS

Paros

Naxos

Antiparos

Chora

Ios

Sikinos

Vathi Bay

Karavostassis

Folegandros

CHAPTER 1
THE STRAIT OF GIBRALTAR

"Thirteen suitcase nukes?" Adam Weldon looked skeptical.

"I'm afraid so," the admiral answered. "On their way to target cities in Europe and America."

"Not good," Tripnee said.

The three of them sat in the center cockpit of the nine-million-dollar, 70-foot sloop, *Dream Voyager*, as it glided on autopilot in light winds under full sail eastward through the Strait of Gibraltar into the Mediterranean Sea. The cliffs of Morocco's Atlas Mountains slid by to starboard, while the Rock of Gibraltar towered to port.

Admiral Ty Jeppesen's motor launch followed in their wake a respectful two hundred yards back, while the United States aircraft carrier USS *Nimitz* followed two miles behind that.

"Why such extraordinary lengths to tell us this in person?" Tripnee asked.

"Because America, Europe, the world, needs your help." The tall, somewhat world-weary admiral, an old Navy SEAL buddy of Adam's, exuded authority and urgency.

Eyes narrowed, Tripnee said, "But we need a break from all that."

"I realize that. The thing is, you're the perfect people, in the perfect position, to quite literally prevent World War III."

Adam asked, "How?"

Tripnee crossed her arms, frowning.

"Back in the 'eighties," Jeppesen said, "as the Cold War wound down, eighty-four portable nuclear bombs the size of attaché cases went missing in the Soviet Union. Just one could devastate a city the size of Paris or New York. If thirteen—or any number—were set off in Europe or America by Iran-backed terrorists, the inevitable response would be to obliterate Iran and who knows what else. Russia, Iran's ally, would counterattack, and we'd be thrust straight into World War III."

"But why me and Adam?" Tripnee demanded, scowling.

"Thirteen of these bombs will soon be smuggled through the Greek islands aboard sailboats—"

"Why sailboats?" Tripnee interrupted. "Why not private jets?"

"Private planes would've worked years ago," Jeppesen answered, "but now, both big airports and shipping hubs, and also smaller airports, have scanners and sensors, and often, bomb-sniffing dogs."

"And sailboats and yachting marinas are still below the radar," Adam said.

"Exactly." Jeppesen nodded.

"You haven't answered my question. Why me and Adam?" Tripnee asked again.

"The two of you sailing *Dream Voyager* look the part. You're glamorous. You'll blend into the Greek islands boating scene."

"Lots of your people can sail. Get them."

"You both speak Arabic."

"Not convincing."

"The real reason?"

"Yeah," she said.

"Okay. The real reason: You're the best."

"Flattery will get you everything. Not."

"Seriously," Jeppesen insisted. "You're both savvy and

resourceful, and deadly when needed. Let's face it, you've had more success taking down conspiracies than anyone else we have."

"Humph." Tripnee glowered, immobile.

"What Ty is too diplomatic to say," Adam said to Tripnee, "is that we're also unofficial, below the radar, and expendable."

"Well," the admiral admitted, "there is that."

"So, if something happens to us, there's full deniability," Tripnee said. "That's some sales pitch."

Adam asked, "So what is the situation?"

"We're looking at a new Islamic terrorist threat group, calls itself the *Jamaat-e al-Aliemlaq*, that operates in the Greek islands." Jeppesen looked out over the sun-drenched water toward the eastern horizon. "Means 'Cyclops Group,' and we think it's a mix of ISIS, al Qaeda, and the Islamic Revolutionary Guard Corps. They're constantly changing, adapting. Iran supplies weapons. To finance their operations, they raid antiquities, arrange for human trafficking, you name it. All manner of dirty, nasty stuff. What's weird, despite being religious fanatics intent on getting into Paradise by imposing Allah's law, the *Shari'a*, on all world, some of them have developed a taste for the good life: sailing, partying, carousing on the idyllic islands of the Aegean. We need to penetrate this group, as soon as possible—no later than yesterday, we've got to identify and track the key operatives and their boats, and find and secure those bombs."

"Spread throughout the Aegean? That's six *thousand* islands," Tripnee blurted out.

"We have leads." The admiral locked eyes with her. "You'll have to be resourceful. Use your wits."

Adam scratched his head and rubbed his chin. And eventually nodded.

Tripnee rolled her eyes and shook her head.

"Also, Interpol is sending an agent who will join you and brief you in Athens. An expert in high-tech spycraft, including electronic eavesdropping and drone facial recognition technology. The latest stuff to give you an edge.

"I won't lie, the slightest slip-up could get you killed. Also, we have constraints. People breathing down our necks. Senators and House people who oppose operations like this. People with no idea of the challenges we face, and no understanding of what's at stake, are ready to hold hearings and scream bloody murder, and even send the three of us to jail if things go wrong."

"Same ol', same ol'," Adam said. "What about the president?"

"We have his full backing."

Adam felt his old friend's stress. The admiral, as a key mover and shaker in the world of US espionage, had always displayed tremendous grace under pressure, but here, within sniper range of the Rock of Gibraltar, Ty Jeppesen's voice and hands trembled with suppressed intensity as he concluded, "The stakes could not be higher. Will you help us?"

Tripnee, eyes narrow, neck muscles corded, rose up and jabbed a finger in front of Jeppesen's face. "How the hell can we say no?" She stormed down the companionway.

Jeppesen signaled his motor launch to come alongside. Before departing, Adam's longtime friend said, "Just so you know: Interpol and the Greek authorities are good, but we're pretty sure they have leaks, and probably a mole. Best not to look to them for any help."

"Good to know."

"Also, you must be getting famous. Interpol specifically requested you."

CHAPTER 2

ATHENS

Five days and 1,640 nautical miles after the admiral's bombshell visit, *Dream Voyager* swept northward across the Saronic Gulf toward Athens. An impossible feat for most sailboats, but an easy romp for Adam's extraordinary craft. The boat, after all, had been specially conceived by acclaimed nautical designer, Bruce Farr, to perform like a Ferrari while providing the luxury of a Rolls Royce.

As Athens came into view, Adam and Tripnee sat together at the helm, marveling at the sight of the Parthenon on the Acropolis towering above the fabled city.

Tripnee said, "The Cradle of Western Civilization."

Nudging her in the ribs, Adam asked, "What about your 'Down with the Patriarchy' campaign? Wasn't this where the patriarchy got launched?"

"Ancient Greece was patriarchal, all right," she said, poking him back.

"And?"

"And they also had plenty of amazing, badass women who didn't take any shit." She jabbed him again, hard.

"That was a badass poke."

"But imagine how this sight must have overawed everyone who sailed into Athens in ancient times—and how it gave pause to anyone thinking about attacking the place."

The Alimos Kalimaki Marina was a madhouse, pulsating with

hustle and bustle. With sails furled, Adam motored deep into the marina's labyrinth of fairways, while Tripnee hung fenders off the stern and along both gunwales. A dazzling collection of gorgeous yachts—all Med-moored, that is, tied up stern-to to the quay—extended as far as the eye could see. Every boat was a beehive of activity, some loading and heading out, others going nowhere, just teeming with people partying.

Finding no open quays, Adam picked a spot where the yachts on either side looked loosely packed. But were they loose enough for him to jostle them aside and force his way in?

He aimed his stern into a narrow opening between two boats, dropped anchor, and powered backward. Tripnee added fenders to both stern corners and readied the mooring lines. The trick was to pry the boats on either side apart without grinding boat-to-boat. Slowly, ever so slowly, with fenders squeezed almost, but not quite flat, the boats to starboard and port shifted aside as he eased *Dream Voyager* farther and farther back until, finally, they were in.

People materialized from neighboring boats to receive their mooring lines, which they passed through rings on the quay, then tossed back to be secured to stern cleats.

Tripnee said, "Good job, Adam, docking the boat. I didn't think it would fit."

Silly, Adam thought, but this simple appreciation meant the world to him.

Tripnee and Adam showered, dressed, closed and locked all hatches, and set the alarms. On shore, first, they checked in with the harbormaster and cleared Greek customs. Next, they visited a nearby supermarket where they filled a taxi with supplies to restock *Dream Voyager*.

After packing everything on board, they again locked up and set the alarms, and again set off, this time deep into Athens.

A thirty-minute Uber ride through teeming, sweltering streets brought them to the edge of the historic Plaka District which surrounded the Acropolis. Here they made their way on foot through ancient, twisting streets no wider than alleyways to a particular outdoor café. Taking seats at a shaded table, Tripnee ordered an ouzo and Adam a coffee. Here, soon, they were to meet their tech-savvy Interpol contact, S.I. Katopodis.

Adam studied their surroundings, his back to a stone wall, his senses alert. A steady flow of people, mostly tourists, but also local folks of all sorts, flowed past.

Tripnee glanced around, then looked up and let out a low gasp when she saw, far above, the Parthenon shimmering in heat waves rising from the city.

Then, off in a different direction, something in his peripheral vision caught Adam's attention. A tiny drone moved slowly along at rooftop level, about fifty feet above them. He pointed it out to Tripnee. As they watched, it swooped down to hover a dozen feet from them, where it did a little dance, swinging from side-to-side, twirling and doing backflips. Then the hummingbird-sized quadracopter shot up, disappearing skyward.

"Why do I sense our tech-savvy Interpol guy is a hot-shot drone pilot?" Adam mused.

"Why do you assume S.I. Katopodis is a man? Could just as easily be a woman."

"You got me." Adam smiled. "Unconscious bias, perhaps. But, I dunno, what do we know? Super tech-savvy. A veteran Interpol undercover operative. A counter-terrorism expert. Speaks five languages. Skilled in hand-to-hand and small-arms combat. Explosives expert. Their top authority on Greece and the Aegean. And, I gather, an experienced sailor, to boot. Pardon me if I say the odds are Katopodis is a man."

"Typical patriarchal chauvinist bullshit."

Just then a tall, very fit-looking woman with wild, luxuriant, shoulder-length blond hair and striking blue-green eyes approached their table.

"Adam and Tripnee? Hi, I'm Agent Katopodis."

CHAPTER 3

SOUNION

"Call me Sophia," the woman said as they all shook hands. Adam gestured for her to sit down, but she remained standing. "Thank the lord you're here," she said with an appealing German accent. "There's no time to spare. We've got to get to Finikas Marina on the island of Syros. I'll fill you in once we're underway."

Tripnee and Adam exchanged glances.

"Well, all right," Tripnee said. "No beating around the bush."

"Amen," Adam said.

An hour later, after helping Sophia and Tripnee move a taxi-load of Sophia's technical gear aboard *Dream Voyager*, Adam checked out of the marina at the harbor master's office.

A wraith-thin, uniformed member of the Greek Coast Guard, a sort of naval policeman, said, for the third time, "Strong *meltemi*. Not possible to go to Cyclades. Saronic Gulf yes. Cyclades, no."

And for the third time, Adam explained, "You don't understand. I sail. I know what I'm doing."

The young Greek kept shaking his head.

Should he just walk away, ignore this petty official, and sail to the Cyclades anyway? Probably not the way to go. Doing this might call attention to *Dream Voyager* just when their mission called for a low profile.

Adam dialed a number, explained the situation, and handed his cell phone to the official. The gaunt-faced Greek coast guardsman spoke briefly, but mostly listened. Two or three minutes later, looking chastened, he handed the phone back, and said quietly, "Sail where you want." Apparently, Sophia had some clout.

Soon thereafter, while Tripnee and Sophia pulled in the stern mooring lines, Adam eased the throttle forward, and *Dream Voyager* crept away from the Kalamaki quay. Oh-oh. The harbor exit was to port, but an errant anchor chain from a neighboring boat rubbed hard against their starboard side rotating them to starboard. Worse, the chain passed close under their keel and looked like it would at any moment disable their propeller.

Adam looked back. A middle-eastern-looking guy on the quay pulled out an Uzi machine pistol. "Gun! Get down!"

Tripnee dropped fast. But Sophia froze. Adam reached out and pulled her down below the cockpit rim moments before bullets hissed by inches over their heads, ripping into the stern bulkhead of *Dream Voyager*'s cabin. The barrage was intense—but brief. Probably one full clip. Then silence.

Adam risked a quick look. The guy had already disappeared along the quay. But who knew if he might return or if there were others?

With Tripnee and Sophia still hunkered low in the cockpit, Adam stood up and accelerated forward, cranking the wheel full to port.

Come on, baby, turn, turn. And don't lose your prop.

But the neighbor's anchor chain wouldn't budge, and *Dream Voyager* swung inexorably to starboard. Amazingly, though, the prop missed the mooring line.

Checking all around for gunmen, Adam realized he was heading straight into a narrow dead end lined with costly yachts. Despite countless near-death encounters as a SEAL, his heart was pounding. Hello, pandemonium. Fortunately, it was clear what to do. But was the fairway wide enough? And more importantly, was he about to be pulverized by another Uzi barrage?

Dream Voyager, in reverse, had what sailors call prop walk to starboard. Adam developed speed along the right side of the fairway, turned hard to port, then, just before his bow hit a majestic yacht on the left side of the fairway, he cranked the wheel the other way and accelerated in reverse. This stopped his forward motion, propelled him backward, and continued the boat's counterclockwise spin. Trouble was, another dazzling yacht loomed a few feet off his stern.

So, all the while wondering if it would be the last thing he ever did, he moved forward and back, forward and back, each time rotating a little more counterclockwise. At last, *Dream Voyager* completed a 180° fairway turn. Then, willing his heartbeat to return to normal, he accelerated through Kalimaki's labyrinth of fairways toward the seawall exit and out onto the Saronic Gulf.

"Thank you, Captain," Sophia said with a broad smile. "You handled that beautifully."

Adam grinned and stood a little taller.

"Who the hell was that back there?" Tripnee demanded, looking at Sophia. "Until you came aboard, everything was fine."

"I wish I knew," Sophia answered. "Things here are tense, explosive. I'll fill you in. But right now, I need to go below."

The wind was dead calm, the temperature still around 90°F, and the water a brilliant, cobalt blue. Motoring eastward at 12 knots, Adam anticipated making Sounion Bay, their intended overnight anchorage, before dark. This would put them in position to make Finikas Harbor on Syros early the next day. As Athens fell away behind them, even as they kept a wary eye out for threats, Adam and Tripnee marveled again at the ever-amazing sight of the receding Parthenon glowing atop the Acropolis high above the city.

To welcome Sophia aboard and give her a feel for the ship, Adam invited her, when she came back on deck, to take the wheel. "Just maintain our current speed and heading. All of us will keep a lookout for other boats."

As he gave her the helm, he practiced the useful naval ritual of saying, "Hands off," and was pleased when she knew to reply, "Hands on."

As Sophia took the wheel, she looked around and sighted over the bow into the distance, seeming to fix their course in her mind.

Meanwhile, Tripnee disappeared below and after a while returned with her prized five-foot-long Barrett M82 sniper rifle. The three of them settled in. Adam got out gel-coat materials and patched the Uzi bullet holes in the cabin bulkhead. Tripnee sat at the cockpit table breaking down, cleaning, and resembling her hefty, lethal, matt-black weapon. And Sophia stood at the wheel doing occasional 360° scans but mostly peering forward at the horizon.

After a while, the Interpol agent said, "So, the situation here in Greece. First some background."

Adam glanced her way and listened up. Tripnee rolled her eyes and remained focused on her M82.

Sophia said, "Greece, which is orthodox Christian, was ruled by the Ottoman Empire for centuries. The empire was Islamic. Greece fought for and won its independence from the empire in eighteen twenty-one, and ever since, the Greeks have exacted systematic revenge against Muslims because they were so pissed at the Ottoman rule."

Tripnee's expression hardened as she hefted her newly reassembled rifle and sighted through its telescopic scope at a point on the Greek coastline a mile or so away, a distance well within the gun's range.

"Muslims," Sophia continued, "have lived in Greece since before the fourteenth century, but are under tremendous threat. They feel Greek policies shame them and destroy their identity."

"Now wait one minute," Tripnee interrupted as she turned, rifle in hand, toward Sophia. "Ottoman rule was no picnic. The Ottoman Turks fined non-Muslims and tried to stuff Islam down Greek throats. The Greeks fought long and hard for their independence, and once they gained their freedom they had every right to assert and reclaim their own culture and their own religion: Orthodox Christianity."

Fire sparked in Sophia's eyes. "The Greeks limit the building of mosques—forcing Muslims to pray in unmarked, makeshift, degrading places, such as converted underground garages. They bulldoze Muslim graves. They restrict the way Muslims can educate their kids. They fine Muslim leaders, the muftis and imams. They even stripped sixty thousand Muslims of their Greek citizenship—an action criticized by the European Human Rights Commission."

Tripnee leapt up. With her feet spread wide on the cockpit bench and her gnarly Barrett M82 at port arms, she towered over Sophia. "Greece has to hold the line against millions and millions of restless Muslims next door in Turkey and just across the water in the Middle East and Africa. If Greeks don't defend their culture—which has contributed so much to the world—it'll get swallowed."

Sophia Katopodis maintained outward calm, but her long, lithe body vibrated with tension as she replied: "Greece treats Muslims like second-class citizens. Muslims in Greece can be both Muslim and loyal Greeks at the same time. Most want nothing more than to peacefully practice their religion."

Adam made a palms-down calming gesture, and said, "How about we agree to disagree?"

It was sweltering hot and Sophia was still fully dressed in a long-sleeved shirt, long pants, and a light, stylish jacket. She seemed to notice for the first time that Tripnee and Adam had changed into laid-back sailor attire: Tripnee wore shorts and halter top and Adam his well-worn shorts and t-shirt. Excusing herself, and returning the helm to Adam, she went below.

After a while, she returned in a two-piece aquamarine *pareo* wrap that made the blue-green of her eyes pop. She twirled on her tiptoes at the top of the companionway. The spin seemed oddly girlish, even vulnerable, for this serious woman.

Tripnee's eyes narrowed at the sight. But for Adam the effect was mesmerizing. He had to look away.

Sophia said, "The problem is that a small group of Muslims have turned to fanatical jihad and linked up with ISIS, al Qaeda, and Iran. Spread through the Greek islands, these terrorists are constantly evolving and adapting. Doing everything they can to mess with, corrupt, disrupt, and destroy life in Greece and the West. What's weird is that some of them have developed a taste for a wild, over-the-top, Western lifestyle: yachting, partying, carousing, and snorting drugs. Having their seventy-two virgins right here in this life. To finance themselves—and to wreak havoc—they traffic in antiquities, drugs, humans."

"You know for a fact they have suitcase nukes?" Adam asked.

"Thirteen," Sophia said. "In shielded cases that block radiation, making normal Geiger counters useless."

"Locations?"

"Strung out across the west Aegean," Sophia said. "A slew of terrorist sailboats getting ready to launch a full-blown, hell-on-earth, jihad holocaust."

*　　　　　*　　　　　*

They dropped anchor in Sounion Bay as, just to their east, the setting sun's last rays lit the majestic Temple of Poseidon on Cape Sounion. Once the anchor was set, first Adam, then Sophia, then Tripnee hit the water, which was a comfortable 77°F. After swimming several laps around the boat, Adam, with Tripnee close behind, climbed back aboard, and headed down to the galley to prepare dinner.

Up in the warm night air in the cockpit, the two served dinner: a feast of spaghetti, meatballs, a huge Greek salad and a smooth red wine. Sophia, who had been puttering in her forward cabin, appeared in her same pareo. Now, however, she also wore glasses and an unusual watch on her left wrist.

"A toast," Adam said, "to this spectacular setting."

They lifted their glasses.

As the trio ate, a small drone like the one in Athens circled the cockpit three times, then darted away.

Tripnee said to Sophia, "Okay, we get it, you're a drone pilot."

"Not just a drone pilot," Sophia said. "A drone falconer. Not just one drone at a time, drone swarms."

Tripnee looked nonplused, while Adam nodded approvingly.

"Watch this," Sophia said as she moved her hands through the air as though operating an invisible control board. Four drones flew out of the balmy night in single file, circled the cockpit, then deftly landed one-by-one on the ship's rear deck.

"Very impressive," Adam said. "How'd you do that?"

"AR, augmented reality. These glasses and this wrist device are a set that allow me to fly an entire drone swarm. While you two do the old-fashioned, actual, physical stuff, my drones, with facial recognition software and more, can identify people and monitor everything they do, including voice and electronic communications."

"Sounds like science fiction," Adam said.

"Oh, it's real all right," Sophia said. "Lots of intelligence agencies and corporations and NGOs are using this same stuff."

Tripnee rolled her eyes, looking unimpressed.

"Think about it," Adam said to Tripnee. "If these devices work, first, Sophia can help us identify people in this *jamaat* conspiracy. Then her drone eavesdropping could give us a crucial edge, almost like reading minds."

Tripnee nodded slowly, her lips pressed into a straight line.

"Drone falconer," Adam said, turning back to Sophia. "Where did you come up with that?"

Tripnee said, "There was a time when royal households had flocks of trained hunting falcons. The person who tended and controlled them was called the falconer."

Sophia said, "That's right."

"How'd you become so adept with drones?" Adam asked.

"By spending too much time with 'em."

"Too much time?"

"Yeah, and maybe not enough with people."

CHAPTER 4

CYCLOPS: MY EYE

My eye. My eye. My missing eye.

I burn like it was yesterday, like it was five minutes ago. But it was long ago.

Poor Papa. He suffered so much. More than me. He told me so. The bomb had to be built. It had to be. Allah willed it.

The kids in Hamburg, then the Greeks on Syros, recoiled from the dark hole in my face, from me. All except Papa. My dear, wonderful papa, who loved me so much. My papa, my Muhammad, may peace and blessings be upon him as he walks and lives.

My papa, my universe, my everything. And I his. He was my shelter, my refuge, and even back then, so long ago, with me so small, I learned to be the same for him.

His pain, his humiliation. He came to Germany as a penniless migrant. Taught himself German and studied computers. Became a brilliant computer scientist. And, praise Allah, he's so charismatic, with incredible, wonderful powers over people. And with such light skin.

Still, the humiliation. Small of stature and Muslim. They shunned him, passed him over. Even when he found a position, he was the last to get promoted and the first to be let go. A slow death by a thousand cuts—to the skin, to the heart, to the eyes.

And then the bomb. I was so small and so proud that he let me help him build it. Who could have known that it would explode and put out my eye! But poor Papa. He cried and cried and screamed because it wasn't possible to take me to the hospital. After all, we had to keep the bomb secret.

The ugly hole in my face—and the unending pain! At first it was so horrible. But what a gift. A gift from Allah. My wound makes me strong. I learned. I understand. Life is pain. Life is sacrifice and submission. I wouldn't have it any other way.

And then back to Papa's family home on Syros where life only got harder—at the hands of the Orthodox Christian Greeks.

Ah, Mama. How she hated life on Syros! A nineteen-year-old rebel beauty angry at her wealthy, conservative father when she met Papa. But deep down, a German do-gooder Christian who took *pity* on Papa and me. Out of that pity that little Ramzi was conceived. How we hated her pity.

Papa taught me and Ramzi tech, and it was me who loved it, not so much Ramzi. I am Papa's tech genius. Back then Papa and Mama fought… and fought and fought. Mama was so unhappy. And so was Papa.

But we will get even. Papa, me, my brother Ramzi, our people, Allah. We will be avenged and we will triumph. The infidels will pay. So, so, so dearly. Allah willing, peace and blessings be upon him.

CHAPTER 5

FINIKAS HARBOR

Early the next morning, *Dream Voyager* weighed anchor and slid past the Temple of Poseidon high on Cape Sounion. Poseidon, the god of the sea and Zeus' brother, was to the ancient Greeks an awe-inspiring and capricious god who at times smashed their long, narrow oar- and sail-powered triremes on the rocks, at times swallowed them whole, and at times provided wonderful smooth sailing. This massive temple, perched on this craggy cape at the southeast corner of continental Europe, built in 444 BC at great sacrifice, no doubt represented a plaintive appeal for that third outcome, the smooth sailing.

For Adam, Tripnee, and Sophia, as they jumped off from mainland Greece and Europe into the Aegean, heading southeast into the fabled Cyclades Islands, the heart of ancient maritime Greece, the cradle of Western civilization, the way was smooth. They glided over a windless and glassy translucent-blue Aegean, through Stenon Kithnou, the strait between the islands of Kea and Kithnos.

The mainland behind them and these islands, with their sparse vegetation and stark grandeur, bore a striking similarity to the lower reaches of California's semi-arid, ruggedly beautiful Kern River Valley. Herodotus himself, Adam reflected, laughing, would have noted the similarity had he been more widely traveled.

They passed a fleet of kaikis, small rough-hewn wooden fishing boats, near the northern end of Kithnos. Each had a line or two in the water, but none seemed to be catching much. Adam was reminded that the whole Mediterranean, in a sad downward spiral caused by centuries of over-fishing, had long produced ever diminishing catches of smaller and smaller fish.

As they motored along over the glassy water, Adam figured this was as good a time as any to get better acquainted with their enigmatic new team member and her drones. He turned the helm over to Tripnee and as he headed down to Sophia's cabin, Tripnee gave him a dagger look that could kill. Women.

Now in a skin-tight yoga outfit, Sophia sat on the floor of her cabin doing stretches and yoga poses. She welcomed Adam in, lighting up with a big smile. Stacks upon stacks of drones and high-tech spyware were piled high against every wall of her stateroom.

Adam surveyed the room. "Look at all this gear."

"Yes. Some very cool stuff."

Intrigued, Adam said, "Yeah? Show me."

Rising from the floor, Sophia slipped a pair of drone control glasses onto his head and a wrist device onto his left arm, and patiently explained their use. As she resumed doing yoga postures, he started practicing with an apparently indestructible little rubber drone the size of a thimble. He crashed it over and over at first. But gradually he got the hang of it enough to fly the tiny device back and forth from one end of the cabin to the other.

"Amazing, these glasses. I'm literally looking out through the drone's camera eyes."

Still down on the floor, Sophia hiked a leg straight up in a gymnast's stretch. "Each drone is a GPS tracking device. You can see what they see, listen, and also track 'em."

"Nice. But what about wind? Can these tiny things fly in strong winds?"

"Believe me, they *are* amazing. This is the latest generation of UAVs, unmanned aerial vehicles. They can fly in just about any weather they're so aerodynamic and powerful."

"Can you really control an entire swarm at once?"

Lowering one leg and raising the other, she cracked a sheepish smile. "Okay, last night I got carried away and was boasting a little. The full answer to that is slightly complicated: They mimic flocks of birds or schools of fish with collision avoidance sensors and bio-mimicry software, so I really can pilot any number of drones. But in tight spaces, it's usually best to fly just one at a time."

Sophia lowered her leg, leaned back on the cabin floor, and rose up in a deep back bend and with hands and feet on the deck, she walked fingers toward her toes until her lithe body was in an impossible upside down U-shape.

With pelvis and stupendous chest jutting skyward, and blond hair cascading to the floor, she said, "An exception is when you entrain them. In that case, I pilot the first drone and the others follow one-by-one. And I can position any number of drones in multiple locations to track and spy on boats, people, you name it."

"When you're flying near people, how do you avoid being seen?"

"That's where years of practice come in."

"I'm impressed." He gestured toward the stacks of drones lining the cabin. "I look forward to seeing these little choppers in action."

Sophia came out of her pose. Her posture was amazing, and her aquamarine eyes so hypnotizing he again had to look away.

*　　　　*　　　　*

Tripnee saw the southwestern point of Syros in the distance a little before noon. They steamed into Finikas, a picturesque bay lined with classic Greek whitewashed, blue-trimmed houses, about half an hour later, just as a light wind picked up, and all three were on deck.

Adam performed a Med-mooring by turning *Dream Voyager* stern-to a stone quay, dropping anchor, and backing into a gap in a row of motley boats. Adam and Tripnee extended the power gangplank from the stern to the quay, plugged in the electric cord, topped off water tanks, and squared away the boat.

Meanwhile, Sophia went below. Soon, nearly invisible drones the size of bumble bees shot up from the open hatch over her cabin.

As Adam and Tripnee set off to explore the place, she slipped her arm through his. Unlike the vast fleet of gleaming, high-end yachts at Kalimaki, the boats here were mostly smaller and humbler. Among a sprinkling of luxury yachts were scores of lateen-rigged dhows, small kaiki fishing boats, and trehantiris. Double-ended with sharp bow and stern, and known as the donkeys of the sea, trehantiris were slow, but good in rough weather.

As they walked the quays of Finikas, Adam and Tripnee stopped to admire a variety of vessels and briefly chat up the people onboard. One powerboat that caught their attention was a magnificent, eighty-foot karavoskara. Traditional Greek deep-sea trading vessels, karavoskaras had the graceful, sweeping lines of the ancient, fabled two- and three-masted caravels that once plied the Mediterranean and far beyond.

Tripnee playfully thrust her chest out and her shoulders back. "Did you know two of Columbus' boats—the *Pinta* and the *Niña*—were caravels?"

Adam pretended to doff his hat and bow. "Did not. I'm duly impressed by my lady's vast knowledge."

As Adam did this, he noticed a scowling face peering out of a porthole and, back behind the face, many, many sets of eyes. Sad, frightened eyes. An angry-looking dark-skinned man with straight black hair banged the porthole shut and closed the curtain. Quite a contrast from the warmth and good cheer of most everyone else in Finikas. And, also, odd because it was the heat of summer—that time of year when sailors kept hatches and portholes open for ventilation.

As he looked at the artfully-built, obviously expensive ship, Adam noted that it was neither a rough, working vessel, nor one dedicated to recreation. It had an austere, stripped-down quality. No commercial fishing or cargo-loading gear. No Bimini awnings, BBQs, paddle boards, windsurfers, jet skis, or bicycles. Not even any swim fins or snorkels—or any of the other toys or frills adorning virtually all the pleasure craft thereabouts.

Tripnee read the ship's ornate name plate. "Interesting boat, the *Al-Gazi*. In Arabic, the name means 'warrior.'"

Adam understood enough basic Arabic to get by, but Tripnee seemed to be forever showing off her superior grasp of the language. Okay, okay. Nothing new about that.

But the *Al-Gazi*. Adam was struck by how the handsome vessel stood out, not for what was happening upon it, but for what was not happening. In a harbor of boisterous boats, the *Al-Gazi* was quiet. Too quiet? It might be nothing, but after countless investigations, Adam had learned to pay attention to intuitive tremors, however faint, and made mental note of the *Al-Gazi*. Had he just glimpsed, through that porthole, hatred? Human trafficking?

As they moved on, Tripnee whispered, "Did you see what I saw?"

"Human trafficking, maybe?"

"Shall we do something?"

"Finding nukes comes first. But later, yes, let's do something about *Al-Gazi*. And there may be a connection."

After a while, thinking of Al-*Gazi*, Adam said, "Seaworthy trouble."

Picking up on one of their favorite word games, Tripnee said, "Solid turmoil."

"Steadfast torment," he said.

"Stalwart tribulation," she said.

"Steady turbulence."

"Stouthearted tumult. Sound topsy-turviness. Sturdy tempestuousness."

Adam laughed "Okay, okay. Once again I bow before my sharp cookie."

As they continued on around the quays, Adam kept an eye peeled for Sophia's drones. But only once did he notice one zip into the stern-most porthole of an elegant yacht. Even though he guessed it had to be a drone, it looked and sounded like an insect.

It was still early afternoon, when, on the other side of the marina from the *Al-Gazi*, Adam and Tripnee came upon *Saadet*, a spectacular 60-foot catamaran sitting low in the water. A wild party was in full swing. Loud, heavy metal blared and colorful drinks flowed. A bartender on the boat's spacious rear patio steadily mixed big cocktails, which were immediately snatched up and gulped down by a gyrating, cavorting group of five muscular, swarthy men in Speedos and two shapely blond-haired women in string bikinis.

A third young bikini-clad blonde lounged, with a big Mojito in hand, on the catamaran's stern a few feet from the quay. As Tripnee and Adam approached arm-in-arm, the woman shouted to Tripnee in a slurred voice, "You've got the hunk."

Tripnee smiled playfully and yelled loudly enough to be

heard over the music, "Hands off. He's mine."

The blonde collected herself somewhat and made an effort to reduce her slurring, "Seriously, you're the cutest couple. Hi, I'm Barbie."

Adam and Tripnee grinned, leaned close to be heard over the music and introduced themselves.

Adam asked, "Where are you sailing?"

"Oh, me and my girlfriends aren't sailors. We're just spending the summer working as cocktail waitresses on the other side of the island." She gestured toward the men behind her. "These guys told us they have this big fancy boat and invited us over."

One of the men came over, stood beside Barbie, and ogled Tripnee with his Speedo bulging.

Barbie said, "Masood, meet Adam and Tripnee. Adam and Tripnee meet—"

Without looking at Adam, the man grabbed Barbie's arm and pulled her back into the oscillating knot of partiers. Instead of resisting, Barbie went willingly and jumped into bump-dancing with Masood to the primal, pounding music.

As they moved on, Tripnee said, "Not to be too know-it-all, but in Turkish, *saadet* means happy."

"Darned ironic. That's one unhappy boat," Adam said, feeling uneasy for Barbie and her friends. Should he have intervened on their behalf? Probably. But they were adults presumably able to make their own choices. And in today's world, for him to take protective action would be guaranteed to appear chauvinistic and even racist. Including in the eyes of his own girlfriend.

Back aboard *Dream Voyager*, and as Adam and Tripnee came down the companionway into the main salon, Sophia burst from her cabin. "I've found one of their boats."

"Great," Adam said, as Tripnee crossed her arms and looked skeptical.

"Watch this," Sophia said, placing a laptop on the salon table. As she tapped a few keys, the screen showed a familiar figure.

"Hey, we just met that guy," Adam said. "Name's Masood."

"Wow, you're good," Sophia said. "My Interpol facial recognition software identifies him as an al Qaeda operative. I flew a tiny drone into his catamaran."

"Good going. You're good," Adam gushed.

Tripnee did her eye roll, opened a closet, pulled out her massive M82, and began cleaning it for the umpteenth time.

As the scene unfolded on the laptop screen, Adam, Sophia and eventually even Tripnee leaned forward, intent on hearing every word, seeing every detail.

A deep, angry male voice, probably from a cell phone speaker, boomed in Arabic, "Partying. Dancing, music, alcohol. What are you thinking?"

"Hey," Masood said, "if Allah gives me these desires, they can't be all bad."

"If Cyclops finds out, you're dead. You dirty yourselves and blaspheme the Holy Prophet."

"The girls are infidels. *Kafirs*. Of no importance."

"Clean and purify yourselves. Your glorious time is upon you. *Inshallah.*"

"Yes, I beg Allah for forgiveness."

Interestingly, the drone camera angle showed that, as he said this, Masood had his fingers crossed behind his back.

"The meeting is set for tomorrow morning at first light. You know the place. Go tonight."

"Yes, praise be to Allah."

"You and your team are our top echelon. We are counting on you."

"Yes, glory be to Allah."

"*Allahu Akbar.*"

Masood put down his phone and the clip ended.

Adam said, "Great work. I knew Masood was a scoundrel. You think these guys will lead us to the nukes?"

"I'm sure of it," Sophia said, arching her back ever so slightly.

Smoldering silently, Tripnee returned to polishing her semi-automatic rifle, while shooting occasional dagger glances at Adam and Sophia.

CHAPTER 6

RINIA

A chime prompted Sophia to check her computer. "*Saadet*'s on the move."

Through a porthole, Adam glimpsed the 60-foot catamaran moving sluggishly out of Finikas Harbor with its party in full swing, music blaring, and bodies gyrating.

"What's the range of that drone's transmissions?" Adam asked.

"Video range is ten miles. Tracking range is about thirty."

"Okay. We'll follow with lights out at a distance of about twelve miles. It's crucial we not lose them, but we can't let 'em see us, either."

When the big catamaran was about twelve miles out, Adam, Tripnee, and Sophia brought in their mooring lines, weighed anchor, and followed, motoring with all lights doused, matching speed with Masood's boat.

The *meltemi* wind the Greek coast guardsman had warned about burst to life. Famous for the mayhem it had caused throughout history, the *meltemi* is a regional phenomenon generated by the temperature and pressure differentials between the steppes of Russia to the north and the Sahara to the south. *Meltemis* typically blast across the Aegean out of the north or northeast during July and August, often reaching thirty knots and sometimes accelerating to even sixty knots. And it was July.

For the time being, the *meltemi* blew at fifteen knots, or about seventeen miles per hour. Excellent. Adam power-winched the main sail up the hundred-foot mast, unfurled the genoa, and killed the engine. The boat's quiet, deep humming soul sang forth. Leaning slightly, it glided gracefully forward. There was nothing like being under sail, nuclear catastrophes be damned.

The *Saadet* sailed erratically with numerous course changes, but overall seemed to be headed for Rinia, a small island adjacent to Delos and Mykonos. Adam, sitting at his navigation desk, opened Rod Heikell's *Greek Waters Pilot*. The definitive sailor's guide to Greece, the hefty volume described and mapped every coastline, island, anchorage, and navigation hazard. Turning to the pages on Rinia, he learned that the roughly five-mile-long by two-mile-wide island, which lay about twenty-six miles due east from Syros, was the legendary birthplace of Artemis, the goddess of the hunt, fertility, and wholesome, life-affirming sensuality.

He also noted that it was apparently uninhabited and riddled with numerous deep, multi-fingered bays and inlets.

As *Dream Voyager* followed *Saadet* east toward Rinia, the *meltemi* gradually built to twenty knots, corrugating the Aegean with five-foot, tightly spaced, white-capped rollers. Curiously for a big catamaran, *Saadet* was making only seven to eight knots on a broad reach, forcing Adam to reduce sail to match the slow speed. Thank God for the tracking device built into that little drone, because *Saadet* had turned off all lights, and it would have been impossible to follow otherwise.

Saadet headed around the north end of Rinia.

Hmmm? A key to this type of work, Adam knew, was to put himself in his enemies' shoes and think like them. As he studied the maps and write-up on Rinia, he realized its isolation and many bays and inlets were ideal places for a clandestine rendezvous away from prying eyes. But why go to the windward, exposed side of Rinia, where finding a sheltered anchorage would be far more difficult?

Of course. It was for the same reason. Especially in this building *meltemi*, virtually any captain with half a brain looking to anchor in the area would seek shelter elsewhere, ensuring the windward side of the island would be all the more isolated—and perfect for their purposes.

Sure enough, Adam's screen showed *Saadet* rounding the northern end of Rinia and turning south along the far eastern, windward side of the island, heading for an anchorage in Skhinou Bay. Whatever was going to go down, whoever *Saadet* was going to meet, Adam wanted to get into position early. So, instead of following around to the north, Adam steered for the opposite, west side of Rinia, for Miso Bay on its leeward side.

Before entering the bay, he started the engine, rolled the genoa and dropped the main into its stack pack. Then, guided by his glowing computer, chart plotter, and depth meter, he motored deep into the sheltered bay to drop anchor far up an inlet.

He found Tripnee in the main salon again cleaning and polishing her sniper rifle, and roused Sophia from deep sleep with a few loud knocks on her cabin door. The three of them gathered around a map of the island at the nav table.

"*Saadet* is right now dropping anchor on the eastern side of Rinia in Skhinou Bay, here," Adam said. "We're tucked away on the west side of the island, here. Separating us is a two hundred-foot-high ridge running along this narrow isthmus, which is maybe three- or four-hundred yards across."

He proposed a plan; they liked it; and the three of them got busy packing. Within minutes, the trio set off through the night, rowing for shore in the dinghy. Maybe, after all, this team could come together in the pinch.

Upon reaching shore, they pulled the skiff up onto the

beach. Using the latest night-vision goggles, they began picking their way up a rock-strewn slope. Twenty minutes later, they entered an ancient, half-collapsed stone hut on the crest of the steep, rocky ridge. Looking down through their night-vision scopes, they saw *Saadet* bucking and tossing at anchor in a place only partially protected from what had become a twenty-five-knot *meltemi*.

There was activity aboard *Saadet*. Adam's heart sank as he looked for but saw no sign of Barbie or her friends. Instead, he saw the men were carrying bags up from below and dropping them into the water. The bags looked small, but based on how the men struggled with them, they were dense and heavy, like sacks of cement.

"I've got to get down there," he said to Tripnee and Sophia. "You know the plan."

The women nodded. Sophia pulled drones from her pack and began sending them off through the night down to the *Saadet*. Most were no larger than wasps and almost invisible.

Tripnee set up her sniper rifle on its bipod stand and laid out extra ten-round magazines. Known worldwide by the nick names "Surgeon" and "Light Fifty," the Barrett M82 was unmatched for its long-range accuracy and fifty-caliber, brick-wall-penetrating firepower. Its rounds were so fast, big, and powerful they made bones explode—turning them into tiny shards which scattered and cut like buckshot inside the body.

Glad he had both a drone fanatic and a top sharpshooter backing him up, Adam threaded his way through the night down the steep rocky slope toward Skhinou Bay. He strapped on fins, battle knife, headlamp, waterproof fanny pack, and his Poseidon underwater rebreather at water's edge, already wearing his wet suit. Lighter and more compact than regular scuba gear, the rebreather was silent, bubble-free and had a much better chance of allowing him to approach the terrorist's boat undetected. Before submerging, he checked in via his encrypted waterproof radio headset.

"They're still dumping," Tripnee said. "Over two hundred bags so far, and counting."

He slid into the water. When he was close, about a hundred feet from *Saadet*, he surfaced to reconnoiter. Abruptly the dumping of the small, heavy bags stopped. Then, after an interval, three larger, elongated bags were tossed overboard. Adam felt sick, guessing their contents.

Saadet then hoisted anchor and motored away, not out to sea, but toward another inlet of the bay. Adam submerged and swam out to the dump site, which was about fifty feet deep. Dreading what he would find, he descended and cut open one of the long bags with his combat knife. There, white as a ghost in the light of his headlamp, was Barbie, a look of horror distorting her lovely face. Grief and anger surged through him. This sweet, naive girl dead for no good reason.

At the hands of animals.

Adam fought down blinding rage. Then he cut open one of the smaller bags and found dozens of gold bars. The bags themselves were made of a durable, high-tech synthetic material that was no doubt impervious to seawater and would probably last for decades.

Adam surfaced. He looked around with his night-vision goggles and saw no sign of the enemy.

Sophia's urgent voice yelped in his earpiece. "What was down there?"

"Just as we feared, the three girls. Also, tons of gold."

"Son of a bitch," Sophia exclaimed.

Tripnee let out a cry.

Recovering, Sophia said, "*Saadet* dropped anchor behind the rocky point just south of you, and a second boat just rafted up alongside them."

Tripnee, no doubt sighting through her sniper scope, said, "The second boat is the *Deniz*. Means 'sea' in Turkish."

Adam swam for the rocky point. To make better time and stay in communication with his team, he stayed more-or-less on the surface, braving the big rollers, stroking up the advancing faces, punching the crests, and body surfing down into the troughs.

Sophia's voice sounded in his earpiece. "Adam, my drones are in the *Deniz*, and I'll patch the audio through to you."

Tripnee, right next to Sophia, blurted out, "Your goddamned drones better be hidden. Don't spook 'em."

"They're very well hidden, thank you. I know what I'm doing. Do you?" Sophia bristled. "We wouldn't have even found *Saadet* or this rendezvous if it weren't for my drones."

"Bullshit. Adam and I spotted *Saadet* first."

Adam groaned. "Focus. Focus. We've got to save the world, remember?"

As he labored through the black, turbulent water, Adam felt rather than heard a murderous silence between the women.

Then the drone audio feed crackled with the sounds of tramping and an occasional loud thump.

"That," Sophia said, "is people carrying bags—probably more gold—from *Saadet* to the new boat, *Deniz*. Okay, back to the drone audio feed."

Abruptly the sounds stopped, and a woman on the catamaran said, "Where's the rest?"

"That's all of it," said a male voice.

"That sounds like Masood," Tripnee whispered.

"Habibi, my dear brother, are you certain?" the woman asked.

"Absolutely."

"What a liar," Sophia whispered.

"The gold is a gift from Allah. As is the money from Iran. All of it is needed to take Allah's fight to the unbelievers," the woman stated.

"Yes, absolutely. *Inshallah.*"

"*Allahu Akbar.* Tell me where the gold came from."

"A bunch of Athenians," Masood said, "including some World War II historians, searched through classified Nazi records and figured out that both a shipment of gold and a U-boat on a secret mission disappeared at the same time near the end of that war. They searched for years and finally found the sunken sub and the gold right here in the Aegean. To stop Greece or the EU bureaucracy from seizing it, they kept their salvage operation secret."

A double-sized wave crashed over Adam's head, drowning out the audio feed. After several shakes of his head, his waterproof headset kicked back in. "...one of their crew was a devout Muslim named Ibrahim whose prayers told him the gold was a gift from Allah, meant to finance Allah's warriors."

"Such a devout and wonderful man," the woman said.

"Yes. And, of course, we had to leave no trace, no way for Interpol or Greek officials or the Americans to track down the gold. So, we killed the entire salvage crew, including Ibrahim. Praise Allah, peace be upon him."

"Well done. May it please Allah." There was silence, then the woman said, "Masood, there is a problem."

"What?"

"Your boat stinks of sex, of orgy. You and your men are wallowing in sin."

"Careful, woman. Watch yourself."

"Habibi, darling, it's me, Roxanna."

"The girls were infidels. *Kafirs.* Of no importance."

"If I was in charge, no problem," Roxanna said, "But Cyclops will have your heads."

"Come to think of it, you *should* be in charge."

"Sssshh. Cyclops has ears everywhere."

In a lowered, earnest voice, Masood said, "You got the Iran money. You cut the deal. You sailed the bombs down through the Bosporus. Praise the Prophet, may peace be upon him."

Also in a lowered voice, Roxanna said, "I do like the way you think, brother."

There was a long silence.

"You open the case like this." Roxanna spoke slowly to the sound of metal latches opening. "Activate the device like so, and set the timer like this. Once activated, only the code will shut it down. Beautiful, no?"

"Glory to Allah. So beautiful," Masood said.

"May it please Allah. *Inshallah*."

CHAPTER 7

SAADET

Adam reached the rocky point, climbed from the water, sat on a rock and, still breathing hard, studied the boats through his night-vision scope. *Saadet*'s anchor was pulling its bows down into the oncoming waves. *Deniz*, a handsome yawl about ten feet longer than *Saadet*, was beginning to move away, headed out into the windswept Aegean.

Tripnee, via their linkup, wondered, "Shall I let loose and blast these assholes to kingdom come?"

"Sounds good to me," Sophia said.

"For once we agree."

"Not so fast," Adam said. "Think of the information these people have. If we take 'em alive, we'll have a way better chance of retrieving all the nukes and rolling up the whole Cyclops *jamaat*."

"There're too many terrorists on that boat," Tripnee said.

"Way too dangerous," Sophia said.

"I think it's doable. The thing is, we've got to wrap up *Saadet* fast, so we don't lose track of *Deniz*," Adam said. "I'm going in."

"No," both women pleaded, but Adam activated his rebreather, and slid into the water.

He surfaced about two hundred feet from the *Saadet*. "What's happening on the boat?"

Apparently resigned to his plan, Sophia said, "They're

bedding down for the night." Then with more animation, "I've done some sleuthing and figured out their names."

"Excellent," Adam said. "Where's each crew member?"

"Two, Abu and Uday, are in the portside forward cabin. Here's a recording of those two a few minutes ago." She turned it on:

"I'm telling you, Abu. Think of all that gold. Let's enjoy it."

"You're not thinking. We pledged ourselves to jihad."

"That was before we found the gold. We promised to fight our jihad so our families would be taken care of. Now we can make our families unbelievably rich."

"Uday! The others will never agree to it."

"Who needs them? All the more gold for us."

The recording ended.

Adam said, "Interesting. And the others?"

"Captain Masood Wahab and his first mate, Jamal Samad, are in the starboard rear cabin. Let's listen in."

At first there was a lot of static, but it cleared.

Masood was saying, "But Cyclops could have us killed at any time. In Cyclops' eyes, we're sinners."

"What about Roxanna?" This second voice had to be the mate, Jamal. "She's a leader. And you two are old friends."

"True," Masood said, "we grew up together like brother and sister, but she's too ambitious. Smart, a go-getter, resourceful, but too much out for herself."

"Ahh, I know what you mean. Too ambitious for a woman."

"Allah has chosen us, brother. Me, you, and our men. *Men.* For the historic, holy destruction of the Great Satan."

"And for untold wealth, enough wealth to finance jihad for as long as it takes."

"We will go down in history," Masood said. "*Saadet* is well-able to cross the Atlantic. *Inshallah*, we will let nothing stop us.

We are destined, brother, to spread Allah's law to the farthest corners of the world."

"And have some infidel fun along the way, *alhamdulillah*."

Sophia clicked off the audio feed saying, "Yuck." After a pause, she said, "The fifth guy, Nadir Khan, is in the portside rear cabin. Get a load of this." The audio feed from the drone in Khan's cabin filled Adam's earbuds with the loud rumble of deep snoring.

Adam said, "Okay. I'm going in. I'll start with Nadir Khan."

Saadet's twin hulls, like those of most modern catamarans, had steps going down to water level at their sterns. Adam carefully pulled himself onto the broad bottom step on the port side. After stowing his rebreather and swim gear in the dinghy that was suspended within arm's reach between the hulls, he pulled out his night-vision goggles and Sig Sauer pistol with silencer from his waterproof bag.

He turned off his ear piece, wondering as he did so if he might later regret it. Adam was glad for the intel from Sophia's drones, but at heart he was old school. He needed to focus on his immediate surroundings, and not be distracted by extraneous info or the ongoing catfight raging between his two teammates. His life and the mission depended on it.

He moved up the steps, confident his soft footfalls would be drowned out by the rhythmic crash of breakers sweeping under the boat. When his head came level with the deck, he studied the stern patio area, the ship's bridge high above it, the main salon visible through sliding glass doors, and a swath of the forward deck. All seemed quiet. How do you take down five muscular men one-by-one, without any of them alerting the others?

A few feet away, the skylight hatch above Nadir Khan's stateroom stood wide open. Adam crept to the opening, heard cacophonous snoring, and peered down on the man lying on his back under a thin sheet. Adam squeezed down through the two-foot-square opening. As his feet came down on the bed, the sleeping figure jerked awake and started to sit up. Adam karate-chopped the side of Khan's neck at its base. The violent carotid knockout punch worked like a charm, and the guy was out cold. Adam silenced and immobilized Khan by hog-tying his arms and legs tight behind his back with duct tape from his bag, and secured a sock in his mouth.

Adam froze. Two sets of bare feet on the deck above him moved toward the stern. Odd. They were quiet, furtive—but also frisky, even playful. Then two muted splashes. Peering out through a porthole, Adam saw two men in the water caressing and kissing. Had to be Abu and Uday.

Adam covered the unconscious Khan with a sheet, and closed the hatch he had just entered. He then silently left Khan's cabin, closing the door behind him, and moved along the passageway to the door of the next, the middle, portside cabin. Testing the knob, he found it locked. Getting out his lock picking tools, all the while listening for the sounds of anyone approaching, he set to work on the mechanism, and had the door open in under a minute. The cabin was loaded to the gills, packed from wall-to-wall and from floor-to-ceiling with weapons, munitions, and explosives—enough to mount a small war even without the nuke. Enough to cause no end of chaos in the name of Allah.

He made his way to the door of the portside bow cabin. Locked. Again, he got out his picking tools and set to work. Wait. What was that sound? He lifted his Sig Sauer and froze, listening, waiting. No one appeared. So, he refocused on the mechanism, and had the door open in under thirty seconds. Letting himself in, he re-locked the door behind him.

A standard feature of big catamarans is an abundance of heads, what landlubbers call bathrooms. *Saadet* was no exception. This stateroom had its own luxury bathroom suite with a spacious standup shower stall, separate toilet compartment, ample sink and counter area and even a clothes closet. The closet was a tight fit, but Adam wedged himself inside and pulled the door shut, with the latch taped so he would not get locked in.

Then, he waited, crammed into the airless cabinet with his head jammed sideways onto one shoulder. And waited. Finally, he detected the barely noticeable sound of bare feet returning along the deck above, and he sensed rather than heard the two men slide down through the overhead hatch.

Someone entered the bathroom, closed the door, and padded over to the toilet compartment. Opening the closet a crack, Adam saw a man in shorts facing the toilet, bracing himself against the wall, peeing. Adam came up silent and fast, clamped one hand over the guy's mouth and with the other delivered a blackout squeeze to the carotid.

Damn. Instead of blacking out, the guy, with the sinewy strength of a wild animal, tried to kick the two of them over rearward. Adam threw a leg back for stability and instead of going over backward, slammed the man's head forward into the wall. Stunned, the guy went slack enough for Adam to fold him down and bang his head again, this time hard against the toilet. Finally out cold, the guy got the same treatment as Khan, and Adam left him trussed and comatose on the bathroom deck.

Had the crashing waves concealed the sound of the struggle? Opening the bathroom door a crack, Adam let out a slow breath when he saw the other man snoring on the bed. This time Adam took no chances and clobbered the guy's noggin hard with the butt of his Sig Sauer. Adam repeated the hog-tying, gagging procedure. Three down, two to go.

He opened the cabin door. Light and the sound of voices filtered down from the main salon. Easing the door closed behind him, he crept along the passageway and up the stairs. Two men sat across a table from one other, Captain Masood Wahhab and the man who had to be his first mate, Jamal Samad.

Seeing no weapons, Adam pulled out his Sig Sauer automatic, climbed the steps, and said in Arabic, then English, "Hands up. Don't move. Move and you die."

The two men slowly raised their hands.

He motioned for them to lie face down on the salon deck with hands behind their heads. The men slowly complied, watching for any opportunity to thwart him. But Adam gave them no opening. After trussing Masood's arms and legs behind the man's back, he did the same to Jamal.

All right. Adam took a deep breath.

"Drop the gun," spat a male voice in a thick accent.

Turning around, Adam saw men bunched together where stairs came up to the salon from the portside hull. Four men— the three he had just hog-tied in their cabins, plus an extremely small, skinny new guy—all aiming AK-47 machine guns at his chest and head.

The new, fourth guy must have freed the others. Where'd he come from? Adam lowered his pistol to the deck, and instantly the men charged forward to pound and slash his head and body with the barrels and butts of their weapons. Soon, gashes on his face and head spurted blood. His vision blurred and the world spun.

"Stop, before you kill him." It was Jamal, the mate, yelling from the floor.

The pummeling slowed but did not stop. Abu and Uday, in particular, kept clubbing Adam with their AK-47s, turning his whole body raw and bloody.

"Stop! We need information!"

Finally, the battering ceased. The new, fourth guy—who the

others called Malik—handcuffed Adam's arms behind his back. Next, Abu and Uday seemed to take extra delight in using long knives to slice off Adam's clothes, gouging and cutting him in the process, leaving him buck naked. Then Malik pushed him into a chair.

Damn, where the hell did Malik come from? The guy must have been holed up somewhere where the drones missed him. Might be Adam's last blunder.

Slow to realize Adam understood Arabic, the men spoke freely as they untied Masood and Jamal. The new guy's name was Malik Draco and he was clearly a devout Muslim. Malik had had no stomach for orgy or murder, and had not wanted any part of the gold horde. So, he'd been sort of on strike and sulking in a small forward cabin. Until, that is, he heard Adam clobbering and tying up his boatmates.

Masood, now freed from his bonds, picked up Adam's pistol and jammed it into Adam's right eye, bulging the eyeball. As he did this, a tiny object no bigger than a bee flew straight into Masood's face, almost reaching his eyes, but Masood swatted it away, sending it skittering into a corner, dead.

In thickly accented English, *Saadet*'s captain demanded, "Who are you? How you find us?"

Adam did not reply. He did, however, with his uncovered eye, see a strange-looking suitcase filling a deep cubby on the far side of the salon. AH HA!

Masood whipped the pistol back and forth across Adam's face, raising new welts, opening more lacerations and sending blood gushing down his neck and chest.

"How you know about us? Who you working with?"

No reply.

"What you know about us? Where you come on board?"

Silence.

This went on. And on.

Finally, Jamal said, "This is getting nowhere. I have a better idea. Better than waterboarding."

Masood again jammed the Sig Sauer into Adam's eye. Khan and Malik pressed AK-47s into his neck. Abu and Uday, smiling, held his legs. And Jamal tied Adam's ankles tightly together with the end of a rope. Then the six men carried Adam out onto the catamaran's stern, ran the rope through a pulley on the end of the boom, wrapped the end of the line around an electric winch, and winched in the line to pull Adam's ankles up and up until he was suspended upside down. Then, on the port, island, side of *Saadet*, they swung Adam out over the water, naked, battered, now with blood flowing from legs to stomach to chest to neck, over the face, into his hair and dripping off his head.

Jamal reversed the winch, lowering Adam into the surging Aegean. When Adam's head went under, he did a hanging sit-up to bring his nose and mouth above the foamy surface. He sucked in air desperately, only to choke as a wave covered his face. Abu and Uday laughed. Jamal let out more line until Adam was submerged to his knees with no way to get a breath.

A distant low bang. Adam disappeared below the surface, leaving a dangling rope end and a cluster of bubbles. As some of the men blasted away with their AK-47s at the bubbles, Jamal's head exploded in a fine shower of blood and bits of bone, leaving a jagged open neck gurgling up blood. Moments later, another distant pop—and Malik's head vanished in a pink mist.

* * *

On the nearby island, in the stone hut at the crest of the ridge, looking down through her M82's powerful night scope, Tripnee studied the catamaran and anxiously bided her time.

Sophia, monitoring the boat through her drones' cameras and mics, narrated Adam's progress, capture, and then torture, driving them both out of their minds.

Saadet was about a half mile away, a distance well within the accuracy range of Tripnee's rifle, and her fifty-caliber rounds could easily penetrate clear through the craft, turning it into a sieve if she really let loose. But as long as Adam was aboard, she couldn't open up without risking hitting the big dope.

The terrorists all came up carrying Adam out into the open, onto the stern poop deck. Still, if she started shooting right then, before she got all six, one or two would have time to put a bullet in Adam. So, she bided her time. Never had seconds ticked by so slowly. Then they hung the poor guy upside down and lowered him into the water. That was her chance. But this was a must-not-miss shot.

Taking her time, she sighted on the rope suspending Adam. Feeling her FBI sniper training kick in, she let out a breath, felt her heartbeat slow and, with steely calm, ever so slowly squeezed the trigger. Bang. The line parted. Her beautiful weapon was so well designed, eighty-five percent of the recoil force was dissipated by the gun itself, saving her shoulder and torso from getting slammed backward.

Then came easier shots: blowing off heads. Quickly, she centered the crosshairs of her scope on the first noggin and squeezed off a round. Bam—the head disappeared. The second head had seen her muzzle flashes in the night and was firing in her direction with an AK47—which, ha, would be hopelessly inaccurate at that range. She calmly centered her scope on the head and caressed her trigger. Pop—the wild-eyed head was no more. Searching for her next noggin, she found none. The *Saadet* men had all scrambled for cover.

* * *

When the line holding him parted and he dropped into the sea, Adam made undulating dolphin kicks—like waves passing through his body—to swim under the catamaran and come up in the airspace under the salon between the twin hulls. Doing his best to focus despite the screaming pain of head-to-toe wounds filled with saltwater, he tucked into a tight ball, knees to his chest and passed the handcuff chain around his feet to bring his hands to his front. Then he untied the line binding his ankles and swam for the starboard stern steps.

He moved up the steps, staying low. Right in front of him was the diminutive Malik, with head gone and neck stump gurgling blood. Crouched in the dark, screened from the salon by the molded steps to the bridge, Adam dug the handcuff key out of the guy's pocket and freed his wrists. Then, scooping up Malik's AK-47 from beside the corpse, Adam inched forward and peered around the molded steps.

Four men in the salon. He fired right through the sliding glass doors into the chest of the nearest guy. Abu. As the guy arched, spasmed and went down, Adam swung the AK47 to strafe Nadir Khan. But Khan stayed on his feet and followed the other two as they dove out of sight down the stairs into the portside hull.

As he fired off several bursts to keep the remaining three guys down, Adam, his wounds screaming, raced into the salon, grabbed the odd-looking suitcase from the deep cubby, and ran back out. Judging by its weight, his instincts had been correct and it was the bomb.

He glimpsed his own reflection in a window in the midst of this wild dash. Although sea-washed, his head-to-foot wounds oozed and flowed, covering him in his own blood.

Thank God Jamal had wanted to keep him alive and conscious, otherwise his wounds would be far worse and very likely he'd be dead.

Bullets whizzed past, missing him by inches. They sure wanted him dead now.

Back hunkered down on the port stern steps, Adam grabbed his rebreather from the dinghy hanging in the stern davits. Not a good idea.

Uday, blind with rage at Adam for killing Abu, stormed out onto the stern deck. His AK-47 roared, but his blast was high, missing Adam's head by inches, but missing. Collecting himself, Uday lowered the muzzle of his AK-47 to zero-in on the center of Adam's chest. At that instant, Uday's head vanished in a puff of red mist.

Astonished to be alive, Adam threw himself into the water with his rebreather in one hand and the nuke in the other. Underwater, he put on and activated the rebreather, while the heavy case took him down and down, better than a weight belt.

*   *   *

Tripnee watched Adam climb the stern steps, unlock his handcuffs, fire the AK-47, and run into *Saadet*'s cabin. She ceased firing to avoid hitting him. Adam emerged moments later, followed soon by the terrorist. Another easy shot. Except the guy moved erratically, and she missed by a hair. Yikes, the guy got off a blast on Adam. Was he okay? Bam. Her next round vaporized the operative's noggin. Adam dove off the boat. *Hope to God he's all right.*

"Masood's at the interior controls, starting the engines," reported Sophia, passing on intel from the two drones still operational aboard the catamaran.

Finally free to let loose with Adam off the boat, Tripnee emptied a ten-round magazine through *Saadet*'s cabin roof, searching for Masood.

The engines came to life. The power windless cranked up the

anchor. The catamaran moved forward, picking up speed.

Tripnee slammed in a fresh clip, and poured rounds into *Saadet*'s two engines. Her M82 was, after all, not only one of the world's best long-range anti-personnel sniper rifles, it was also designed to destroy airplanes, vehicles and, yes, boats. Soon, smoke and flames poured out of the hatches over the engines.

But the boat kept moving. Tripnee emptied magazine after magazine, sending a fucking holy hell of lead down onto the bastards. Soon flames poured from every hatch and bullet hole, and an ongoing thunder of detonations ripped giant holes in the boat, blowing away whole sections. Then, when *Saadet* was about a mile out, a single massive explosion obliterated what was left of the vessel, leaving nothing but bits of floating debris.

Sophia, smiling, looked at Tripnee. "Hell hath no fury like that of Tripnee."

So, maybe this bitch isn't so bad. Maybe, Tripnee thought.

It was almost daybreak, and, for an hour as the sun rose, Tripnee searched the area with her powerful scope while Sophia's drones did likewise. There were no survivors. The entire *Saadet* crew was dead.

*   *   *

Back aboard *Dream Voyager*, as both Tripnee and Sophia treated his wounds, Adam said, "You were both right."

"About what?"

"That was too dangerous."

"Well, working together we pulled it off," Sophia said.

"All that for just one nuke," Tripnee said.

"One down and twelve to go. Yikes," Sophia said.

Adam asked, "Any chance we can catch *Deniz*?"

"A drone-tracker showed *Deniz* heading in the direction of Syros," Sophia said.

CHAPTER 8

ERMOUPOLIS

The *meltemi* rose to thirty knots and kept climbing, churning the Aegean into a vast tumultuous landscape of howling waves and airborne foam. Flying a reefed main and half its genoa, *Dream Voyager* flew along at fourteen knots on a close reach headed westward back toward Syros, following in the wake of *Deniz*. Sure, multi-hulled sailboats, that is catamarans and trimarans, tended to be lighter, and faster, at least downwind, but they were no good in rough weather like this. For Adam, nothing surpassed the grace, beauty, and smooth motion of a mono-hull. Like a Roman arch, the classic streamlined shape of *Dream Voyager* steadied by its weighty keel stood up to, embraced, and danced among the untamed elements, among the wild, brutal forces of nature.

"All that Nazi gold," Tripnee mused.

"No wonder *Saadet* was so low in the water and sooo slow," Adam said, as he inspected his raw, painful ankles.

"Enough to direct the course of the future."

"Especially in the wrong hands."

"But in the right hands, think of it."

"Figuring out the ownership of that gold is a problem for the European Union high court," Sophia said. "Making sure it doesn't just disappear into the secret bank accounts of corrupt EU or Greek officials won't be easy."

"How do we do that?" Adam asked.

"Until we track down those nukes, I say we tell no one and leave the gold right where it is."

"Enough said." Adam nodded.

Then, after a pause, Tripnee did likewise.

As the day wore on, despite *Dream Voyager*'s excellent speed, they picked up no signal from the drone aboard *Deniz*. Roxanna's 70-foot yawl was many hours ahead of them and could be anywhere, but finding it was their best hope to track down the other nukes.

Tripnee, head down in the shelter of the dodger at the cockpit table, was once again breaking down, cleaning, and reassembling her M82. Meanwhile, a dozen feet away, Adam and Sophia stood together at the binnacle nav screen looking at a chart of the Cyclades Islands, talking over their options.

"When *Deniz* sailed out of range of the drone's signal," Sophia said, "it was headed straight for Ermoupolis, on the east coast of Syros."

"But we're close enough now to Ermoupolis to re-acquire the signal if they were here," Adam said. "Which probably means they're not here."

"Agreed. The thing is, Syros and Ermoupolis are central to the Cyclades and so maybe to the Cyclops gang? This is the best place to lie in wait and pick up their scent."

"Lying in wait for a while, and having some time for Adam to heal sounds good to me," Tripnee said.

"Hey," Adam said, wincing, "my wounds look worse than they are. I'm fine."

Tripnee rolled her eyes.

"Before long, they'll resurface right here," Sophia said. "Trust me."

As Ermoupolis, the "big city" on the east coast of Syros, drew near, they lowered the main and furled the genoa. Sophia took the wheel, while Tripnee prepared mooring lines. Adam played the invalid, kicking back on the cockpit cushions, taking in the scene. Sophia steered them through the large industrial outer harbor, and then into the historic, sheltered, inner harbor where she performed an expert Med-mooring, backing up to an ancient quay lined with lively tavernas. With the help of people on shore, Tripnee secured their mooring lines to bollards inches from outdoor tables packed with boisterous patrons drinking and dining al fresco.

They took naps. Then, early that evening, in an effort to get Tripnee and Sophia to further bury the hatchet, Adam said, "How about we forget about *Deniz* this evening? Let's relax and explore."

Ermoupolis, it turned out, was a quintessential Greek Mediterranean scene. As the administrative and cultural capital of the Cyclades Islands, the place hummed with vibrant nightlife. The historic quay and surrounding ancient inner city teemed with vacationing Athenians and swarms of travelers from every corner of Europe and the world.

Selecting at random a quaint, outdoor café, Adam, Tripnee, and Sophia sat down at an inviting table festooned with a red-and-white checkered table cloth. The food and drink turned out to be delectable. Wine and talk, and eventually ouzo and laughter, flowed.

"Here's to the ancient Greeks who founded Ermoupolis," Adam said, lifting his glass while doing his best to conceal his head-to-toe pain. "They knew what they were doing. Even though the *meltemi* is raging at thirty knots out over the water, here we're in the lee of a mountain and it's calm and balmy."

Smiling, letting their hair down, they drank toast after toast.

"Hey, we survived *Saadet.*"

"Here's to your drones."

"Here's to your sniper rifle."

"Speaking of that amazing rifle," Sophia said to Tripnee, "how'd you get so good?"

"FBI sniper training helped, but I really learned to shoot with my father. He was a Choinumni shaman in California and a very big deal in our tribe. Hunting was our special, private time together," Tripnee said, smiling with the memory—and no doubt soaring from the booze.

Sophia went silent and distant. Then, wiping a tear from one eye, said, "I'm sorry. I don't know what came over me."

Adam touched Sophia's hand. "Are you okay?"

"I'm fine." Sophia wiped away another tear, and smiled weakly. "I love my father more than life."

With this, the trio grew silent, perhaps with each lost in their own memories.

Later, high from the wine and ouzo, they strolled arm-in-arm through the narrow, marble-paved streets of Ermoupolis.

Nothing like good food and booze for camaraderie. Certainly eases the pain of getting half beaten to death, too, Adam thought.

Back on the quay, they moved along in the steady tidal current of humanity flowing along the waterfront. As they neared their boat, Adam looked ahead through the crowd. A magnificent yawl was backing into the slot next to *Dream Voyager*.

It was the *Deniz*. As it backed in, people on its stern were getting ready to throw mooring lines ashore, and a knot of people on the quay gathered to receive them.

Sophia immediately spun around, turning her back to the docking boat.

Suddenly on high alert, Adam scanned the mass of humanity in the vicinity of *Deniz*. Before him, he realized, sprinkled through the crowd, was a small army of armed men and women. The men were easier to identify with their searching eyes and more obvious bulges under tighter-fitting clothing. The women, their loose flowing clothes better for concealing weapons, were harder to spot——but their swiveling heads and wary, roving gazes gave them away.

"This place is swarming with Cyclops operatives," Sophia hissed in an urgent whisper, as she zipped her collar up over her chin and pulled her jacket hood down in an attempt to hide her face. "ISIS, al Qaeda, IRGC. I've been tracking these bastards for years. Some might ID me."

"We've got to get you aboard *Dream Voyager* without them seeing you," Adam whispered. "I've got an idea."

Ignoring his still painful wounds, with Tripnee following close behind him, Adam stepped through the crowd, outright shouldered one guy aside, and next subtly edged away two more guys who were about to receive *Deniz's* starboard mooring line. Then, just as the line was thrown, he grabbed it and bellowed, "Welcome. We'll help get you moored."

Following his example, Tripnee grabbed the portside mooring line while yelling, "Welcome. We'll help. Welcome."

Their strange, brash, "welcoming" behavior drew all eyes. Virtually everyone, Cyclops operatives and innocent civilians alike, were momentarily flummoxed trying to figure out the intentions of these crazy Americans. Meanwhile, unnoticed on the next boat over, Sophia slipped aboard *Dream Voyager* and quickly disappeared down the companionway.

CHAPTER 9

CYCLOPS: JIHAD

"Seek out your enemies relentlessly." —Qur'an Surah 4:103.

"Believers, make war on the infidels who dwell around you." —Qur'an Surah 9:121.

"Make war on them until… God's religion shall reign supreme." —Qur'an Surah 8:36.

"Slay the idolaters wherever you find them, take them captive, and besiege them" —Qur'an Surah 9:5.

"Fight those who believe not in Allah… until they pay the jizyah with willing submission, and feel themselves subdued."—Qur'an Surah 9:29.

"Study Surah 9:29. 'Subdued' is the key. Nonbelievers must be brought down, made submissive. The only way to do that is to cut off the malignant head and replace it with a caliphate. Notice how this is not a command to fight in self-defense, but an absolute command to attack anyone and everyone who has different beliefs. This famous surah in the Qur'an led to centuries of glorious conquest, and, *inshallah*, it will inspire many more." —Cyclops

"The Great Satan, America, and the whole cursed Western infidel world is a morally decayed culture ripe for Islam. Every day without a caliphate is a sin. Besides, Islamic prosperity depends on conquering new lands and converting new Believers at the point of the sword." —Cyclops

"If you want to change the world, you have to do it through jihad, through the AK-47, through nuclear bombs, through any and all means that Allah, in his infinite wisdom, makes available to us." —Cyclops

"Jihad is incumbent on all. This is why Islam is greater." —Ibn Khaldun

"Muhammad called for the subjugation of the entire world." —Cyclops

Allahu Akbar. God is Greater.

CHAPTER 10
THE ZORBA DANCE

Deniz was no sooner docked, than slow, inviting mandolin and bouzouki music floated across the quay. Adam and Tripnee moved toward the sound. The already burgeoning crowd on the quay swelled as people poured off boats up and down the shoreline. Measured, smooth Zorba music seemed to intoxicate the no doubt already inebriated mass of humanity. A line formed. Adam and Tripnee, to blend in and observe from the middle of things, let themselves be pulled in. They and a hundred other buzzed souls with hands on their neighbors' shoulders moved to the delirious music.

For a long time, they moved slowly, so slowly, savoring each lift of the foot, each shift in weight. Gradually—after ten minutes—or was it an hour?—both the sirtaki music and the press of humans gathered speed, until they moved in a blur, hopping and leaping in unison, as though possessed by a mass euphoria.

Were they dancing with Cyclops members? Not exactly. The wary-eyed people with concealed weapons bulging under their clothes were mostly hanging back. Wily and opportunistic, they had spread themselves out through the crowd of onlookers in order to hide in plain sight.

As the night wore on, the more advanced dancers split into two factions and the whole shindig became a sort of dance off. A wild, cavorting competition raged on the floor and on the table tops of the taverna adjacent to *Dream Voyager* and *Deniz*. First, one team danced, then moved aside. Next, the other group came forward and stepped things up, raising the ante, pouring it on, escalating the moves, outdoing their brethren, only to be outdone in turn by the opposing dancers. And so, this amazing spectacle of sizzling rhythmic agility went on and on, with neither crew having the slightest intention of letting the other get the best of them.

Eventually, Adam and Tripnee withdrew and descended below deck aboard *Dream Voyager*. They found their boatmate in the main salon, engaged in drone falconry.

Sophia pointed toward the quay. "There's a ton of armed terrorists mixed into the crowd out there."

"No shit," Tripnee said. "What are we going to do about it?"

"For the moment, nothing," Sophia said.

"What's happening aboard *Deniz*?" Adam asked.

"They're having one hell of a high-level meeting. Boat captains each with their own fleet." Sophia tapped the keys of her laptop. "I've been recording. Get a load of this."

As a drone's-eye-view video of the gathering in the boat next to them came into focus, six people sat around a handsome table.

"Cyclops is too secretive," said a giant, athletic woman with big shoulders. "Keeps us in the dark."

"That's Sahiba Mukadder, captain of *The Crescent Moon*," Sophia said.

"Cyclops is a *kafir*. We've got no leadership. We're not doing anything," said a tall, dark, thin, bearded man. "We're soldiers for Allah. Let's move. Let's attack in the name of Allah."

Stopping the tape for a moment, Sophia said, "The gung-ho guy is Dogu Kubilay, captain of the *Bora*."

"Praise Allah, we are in agreement," said a small, intense, animated woman with huge eyes and a mouth crowded with big teeth. "We can't wait for Cyclops. We must attack the West now. With everything we have. As hard and as fast as we can. May it please Allah and the Prophet."

"That's our old friend and next-door neighbor, Roxanna Tehranni," Tripnee said.

"Exactly," agreed Sophia.

"Holy war!" Dogu yelled.

"*Allahu Akbar!*"

"Cyclops may, or may not, have a master plan, but we cannot sit idle any longer. *Inshallah*, we must act," Roxanna said. "So, here's our plan—"

Dogu blurted out, "Allah gave us brains to innovate, improvise. Make jihad."

Roxanna continued, "Each of you will get a nuclear bomb and a glorious treasure trove of other weapons and explosives."

Adam noticed that as Roxanna said this, she glanced at a closet door secured by a heavy padlock.

"We've converted the gold into dollars and Euros," Roxanna continued. "There is money for all. Each of you will get an encoded message detailing your assigned targets. The bigger, faster boats will attack America, the smaller, slower boats will perform glorious deeds in Europe."

"I trust we will not overlook the west coast of America?" This from Dogu.

"May it please Allah, peace be upon him," Roxanna said, "the fastest boats of all will sail to the Gulf Coast of America and their crews will travel overland by car and truck to devastate the heartland and the West Coast of the Great Satan."

"May Allah guide us. How will we stay in touch?" asked a bald-headed fat guy.

"That's Galen Hakimi, captain of the *Profit*," Sophia said.

"We won't," Roxanna said. "That's one thing Cyclops did right. We must stay compartmentalized, separate from one another. That is why this is the biggest meeting we'll ever have. When too many of us come together at one time, it's too dangerous. We create too big a target."

"But none of us knows the whole picture." It was Galen again. "None of us knows the location of all of the nukes, of all of the money, or all of the weapons or boats."

"That's how it has to be," Roxanna said. "Except for Cyclops, no one, not even me, knows the whole picture. Each of us will continue to have only one or two contacts outside our immediate cell. That way, if we get captured or compromised, we can't reveal what we don't know."

Dogu said, "I would never give up sensitive information."

"Believe me," said a small, bald man with large eyes and ears, "no one can stand up to serious, prolonged torture. You will talk. Interpol, and the Americans especially, are diabolical devils. They'll stop at nothing to thwart the will of Allah. Peace be upon him."

Pausing the tape, Sophia said, "That's Abdul Kareem Aziz. I haven't figured out if he captains a boat or what. But he's some kind of Cyclops honcho." Then the tape resumed.

"Reminds me of Yoda," Tripnee said.

"Make no mistake," said the portly Galen, "Cyclops has ears everywhere. Cyclops set all this in motion and will always be many steps ahead of everyone. Mark my words, going ahead without Cyclops will not turn out well."

"Cyclops has failed us," Roxanna said. "In the name of Allah, we cannot worry about Cyclops. We are moving forward on our own."

"*Allahu Akbar!*" many voices agreed.

"Don't worry," said a scowling, bearded, dark-skinned man with straight black hair as he rose up and spread his arms wide, "Brothers and sisters. Go forth into Europe and America and wreak havoc. Remember, be selfless and relentless. Adapt.

Innovate. Create chaos. May it please Allah. Peace be upon him."

"I remember that guy," Adam said. "In Finikas Harbor, I saw him through the porthole of that eighty-foot karavoskara, the *Al-Gazi*."

"Yes, very good," Sophia said, "That's Basham Bilel, captain of the *Al-Gazi*."

Tripnee, standing up, closed her hands into fists. "I'd like to take my rifle up onto a roof top and start picking off these sons-a-bitches."

Sophia rose to square off against her. "There're just too many of these fools mixed in with too many civilians to even think about a fire fight."

Adam said, "Even if we could snap our fingers and capture them all right here, that wouldn't secure the nukes. Cyclops, whoever that is, is damned clever. With information so dispersed, not even all these guys put together know the location of all the nukes."

"The only way to get every bomb," Sophia said, "is to keep tracking these guys as they spread out to pick up the nukes. We'll have to catch 'em and collect the nukes one at a time."

Adam looked at Sophia admiringly. "Jeppesen knew what he was doing, adding you to our team. Who else could surveil, plant tracker bugs and drones, and have any realistic chance to round up so many nukes?"

"It's still a fucking long shot," Tripnee moaned. "The consequences of missing even one are unthinkable. And we've got twelve to go."

The plotters plunged into prolonged prayer aboard *Deniz*.

Out on the quay, the Zorba dance-off was going stronger than ever, and felt like it might go on all night. As the two factions took turns outdoing one another on the tabletops, the shindig reverberated far and wide—including through every inch of *Dream Voyager*. Only in Greece. What a people.

CHAPTER 11

ABOARD DENIZ

Sophia woke Adam and Tripnee at three in the morning. The two had only gotten a couple hours of fitful sleep and that with the aid of earplugs.

Sophia herself had stayed up the whole night, monitoring and recording every minute of the terrorist's gathering, no doubt hoping for clues that would locate the nukes.

"The dance off on the quay and the praying aboard *Deniz* are winding down. We've got to decide what to do. The boats around us left, leaving *Deniz* and *Dream Voyager* alone on the quay." Sophia was bone weary but carried on. "Any minute now the terrorists will scatter in every direction. I can follow only one at a time. What do you want me to do?"

"*Deniz* is exactly one foot away," Tripnee said. "After the other terrorists leave, I say we take Roxanna and her crew off the chessboard."

"Easier said than done," Adam said, looking out a porthole at their next-door neighbor. "But we would have the element of surprise."

Tripnee climbed the companionway stairs, poked her head up for a look around and came back down. "We've gotta be quick and decisive. None of this tying-people-up stuff."

Looking at Sophia, Adam asked, "Can you tell us the exact location of everyone aboard *Deniz*, and at the same time track Dogu Kubilay?"

"I'll do my best," Sophia said. "Why Dogu?"

"They're all bad news," Adam said, "but I've got the feeling Dogu's the most gung-ho, the most dangerous."

Sure enough, in the next half hour, the terrorist ring leaders filed off *Deniz*. The leaders, their lieutenants and bodyguards, and the last of the Zorba dancers and hangers on, filtered away in different directions, leaving *Deniz* and the quay quiet. Soon, the drone video feeds from aboard *Deniz* showed Roxanna Tehranni and her crew bedding down, probably exhausted.

Adam selected two Glock 19s with silencers. He made sure the clips were fully loaded and both had bullets in firing position. Through long practice he had taught himself to be ambidextrous and could shoot with either hand, though at long range he was slightly more accurate with his right. At close range, he was equally deadly with either. Tripnee went with two Beretta Picos with built-in lasers and screw-on silencers. Small, light, lethal weapons perfect for the job at hand. Both carried extra ammo clips, and wore body armor, dark clothing, earpieces, and night-vision goggles.

They went into *Dream Voyager*'s main salon, and on the big table saw that four laptops displayed split screen video feeds from eight tiny drones spread through *Deniz* and out on the quay.

Sophia spoke to them through their earpieces to describe the situation on the boat next door: "They've got a big guy guarding their gangplank. Roxanna and her first mate, in more ways than one, Majid Hakami, seem to be asleep in the stern captain's cabin. Another guy is sleeping alone in the first cabin forward of the salon. Two women are snoring in separate bunks in the crew cabin forward of the galley."

Adam whispered into his mic, "Does the sentry seem alert? Which way is he facing?"

"He's awake, but I don't see him turning or looking around

much," Sophia said. "He's facing the quay."

"I like it," Adam said. "Probably assumes any threats will come from that direction."

Adam and Tripnee were poised, ready to move, awaiting Sophia's go ahead. Adam would start at the stern, Tripnee at the bow. The quay was empty as far as the eye could see. The people aboard *Deniz* were asleep, and their sentry had his back to the boat.

Everything looked like a go. Sophia took in a breath, ready to give the signal. But something made her hesitate—and thank God she did. "Oh-oh. A couple is coming."

The couple, strolling arm-in-arm, took forever to pass and move off into the distance. Finally, the coast looked clear, when Sophia again drew in a breath to say go. But instead blurted out, "Wait. A policeman."

The Greek cop came sauntering along and paused to light a cigarette. After an eternity, he moved off and turned a corner some ways off.

Finally, Sophia gave the signal. Adam had one flash-bang grenade and Tripnee had two. They pulled all the pins simultaneously, so all three would go off at the same instant. Adam dropped his through the hatch over Roxanna's captain's cabin, and an instant later took aim at the back of the head of the sentry on the gangplank. *Psst, psst.* A nice double-tap and the guy dropped dead face down on the plank.

Tripnee tossed her first flash grenade in through the porthole where the guy was sleeping alone, then she moved quickly and silently forward along *Dream Voyager*'s deck to toss her second flash-banger through a porthole of the cabin of the two women. She yanked off her night-vision goggles, and covered her eyes and ears just in time for the muffled explosions inside *Deniz*.

Immediately after the explosions, Tripnee pulled her night goggles back on, whipped out her pistols, stepped onto *Deniz*, and dropped prone onto the forward deck. She looked down into the crew cabin at the two women. *Psst, psst.* A bullet into each noggin. *Psst, psst.* Then a second round into each head to be sure.

She then dove head-first down the hatch, rolled off a bunk, and came up on her feet already moving toward the cabin where the male terrorist had just been rudely awakened, doing her best to get there before he recovered from the flash.

A moment after the flash-bangers went off, Adam redonned his night scope, pulled out his silenced Glocks, and ripped open the hatch over the stern master cabin. There was Majid stretched out on a double bed, just now reacting to the flash bangs. *Psst, psst.* Two bullets penetrated the guy's broad forehead.

But where was Roxanna? The other side of the double bed was empty. *Ah ha.* Movement off in a corner. Then Roxanna darted into the head, and the door slammed shut. Adam dropped through the hatch and sent a pattern of slugs through the thin door. Anyone in there had to at least be wounded. And very likely dead.

Uh-oh. On this boat, the master head probably had a door into the engine room, which no doubt had a hatch up into the cockpit. Adam bounded from the cabin, along the passageway, and up *Deniz's* companionway, headed for the cockpit.

Splash. *Damn. Too late.* The engine room hatch stood open and Roxanna was overboard. Adam searched around the boat but she was nowhere to be found. The intrepid little jihadi was no doubt at that moment swimming away underwater, escaping into the night.

Tripnee got to the remaining male's cabin door. Locked. With no time for anything else, she put two bullets into the mechanism, shattering it. She kicked the door in. The guy was dazed but moving, reaching for his AK47. *Psst, psst.* Two slugs entered the man's temple. His sinewy body collapsed like a marionette with the strings cut.

Immediately after giving up the search for Roxanna, Adam checked to make sure the coast was clear, went to the gangplank, carried the sentry's limp body back along it and down into the main salon. As he lowered the corpse onto a couch, Tripnee also entered the salon and the two exchanged glances. Thank God, she was okay. What a woman.

"Roxanna got away."

"Well, we got the rest of them. Thank God, you're okay."

There was no time to spare. Adam blasted open the padlocked closet he'd seen earlier. Sure enough, inside there it was: another suitcase nuke. He also found four duffle bags stuffed with bundled US and Euro currency, and a substantial armory of weapons, munitions, and explosives.

Next, they searched *Deniz* from bow to stern, checking every compartment and nook and cranny. They uncovered three more weapons caches, but no more nukes. They also discovered and bagged a cell phone and a laptop, key material that might help roll up the Cyclopean terrorist group.

Grabbing the nuke, money, cell phone, laptop, and a few choice items from the weapons caches, they climbed the companionway, jumped back across to *Dream Voyager* and went below. Amazingly, the whole operation had taken less than fifteen minutes, though it seemed much longer.

"I'm so glad you're all right." Sophia jumped up, gave Adam a big full-bodied hug, and planted a huge kiss square on his mouth. "We're in luck, I tracked Dogu Kubilay's boat, *Bora,* a little while ago headed south like a bat out of hell. He's got one fast boat."

Sophia flew her swarm of drones back aboard. Adam brought in the stern mooring lines. Tripnee, smoldering, started the engines, powered forward and activated the windlass to bring up the anchor. As *Dream Voyager* slid out of its spot at the quay, Adam pulled the pin of an incendiary grenade with a time delay fuse and dropped it through an open porthole on *Deniz*. When they were two hundred yards away and picking up speed headed out of Ermoupolis Harbor, *Deniz* burst into flames, lighting up an early dawn.

CHAPTER 12
PAROS

Following the last known path of Dogu Kubilay's 70-foot Catana catamaran, *Bora*, Adam, Tripnee, and Sophia pressed south toward the island of Paros across a roiling, foam-strewn Aegean. *Dream Voyager* overtook tightly spaced, twelve-foot rollers one after another. Its sleek hull slowed slightly as it climbed the crests and accelerated as it slid down each face. They moved as though one with the wind, sailing straight downwind wing-on-wing, making their cockpit an oasis of calm, while all around the *meltemi* whipped the sea white.

"Damn." Sophia slammed her fist on the table. "The drone signal from Dogu's boat has vanished."

"Little piece of junk," Tripnee said without looking up from her rifle ablutions, the muzzle of which was angled in Sophia's direction.

Sophia, for her part, arched her back and pointedly spoke only to Adam. "I'm picking up chatter about some kind of *mujahideen* rendezvous in Naousa Bay on Paros. We'll find Cyclops jihadis there, and probably Dogu, too, since I'm sure he was headed that way."

"Sounds good."

Adam tuned out the tension between his boatmates, ignored his wounds, which still hurt like hell, and attempted over and over and over to unlock the *Deniz*'s laptop and cell phone. Every password, every PIN flopped.

After hours of frustration, he endeavored to treat himself to a moment of uplift: They *had* found another nuke. But the formidable Roxanna had gotten away, and their ordeal had only just begun. Without a doubt the worst was yet to come.

So much for the uplift. He went back to code-breaking.

*   *   *

Adam knew from Heikell's *Greek Waters Pilot* that numerous treacherous rocks and reefs surround Paros, one of which, Portes Rock, sank a ferry in the year 2000, drowning 80 souls. As the mountainous 9- by 13-mile shape of Paros grew from a faint blur on the horizon into a distinct landscape, Adam made out key landmarks and steered a course for Naousa Bay, on the northeastern corner of the island. At the bay's mile-wide, north-facing entrance, they lowered the mainsail, furled the foresail, and continued under motor power.

As they crossed the broad, emerald-green bay, they watched for and carefully avoided navigation hazards. Also, they kept an eye peeled for any sign of Dogu Kubilay's distinctive *Bora*, or any other terrorist boat, but saw none. Instead, luxury resorts, Greek Othodox chapels, and the picturesque ancient Greek town of Naousa lined the bay. And Sophia pointed out three sheltered nude beaches while flashing big smiles at Adam.

Adam maneuvered into the quaint, tiny, Naousa marina. Low break waters, which included the ruins of an ancient Venetian fort, protected the small harbor from large swells, but left it exposed to the fierce *meltemi* blasting down through the broad mouth of the bay. It being early in the day, there was lots of space at the quay. Adam turned stern-to, dropped anchor, and backed to within three feet of the stone dock and this time Sophia did the mooring lines.

Where were Dogu Kubilay and his fighters? Adam suggested

Sophia send out drones to run a search, while he and Tripnee climb the mountain behind the town to scan the bay with binoculars.

"We'll stay in touch via our earpiece radios," he concluded. "If we see something, the drones can check it out close up."

Sophia frowned, but said, "Sounds good."

Adam and Tripnee packed powerful binoculars. He put his with a Glock in a day pack, while she put hers, plus her two Beretta Picos, in a fanny pack. Even though it was early morning, the rustic beach resort town of Naousa already thronged with lithe, tan Europeans.

At an open-air restaurant on the waterfront, Adam picked up dolmas, falafel, gyro sandwiches, and a bottle of local wine. Their mission was of overarching importance, of course, but maybe with a little luck he and Tripnee could carve out some time just for themselves. An interlude to clear the air, reconnect, recharge, rekindle the fire, the magic between them. He sure needed it, and he sensed she did, as well.

Case in point: Tripnee seemed increasingly remote as they walked up through the town. Instead of feeling enchanted by the steep, narrow, marble-cobbled streets and timeless, white-walled, blue-trimmed houses, the place, the whole world felt flat and empty. As the town fell away behind them and they climbed higher and higher up the mountain, his heart just got heavier.

He said, "Let's talk."

"Don't you see what's going on?"

"Help me understand. See what?"

"We can't trust that bitch. There's something about her. She's up to no good."

"I don't see it. Where's the evidence?"

"I'm telling you she's toxic, she's covert, she's devious."

"How so?"

"I'll tell you a dirty little secret: Women are just as capable of evil as men, but women are much, much better at getting away with it."

"Can you give me specifics? Spell it out?"

"Well, for one thing, she's playing you. Whenever you're around, she shakes her bottom. Whenever you look her way, she arches her back to thrust out her boobs. And that damned near transparent pareo. And you eat it up."

At that moment Adam noticed a tiny drone hovering ten feet off the ground fifteen feet away, close enough to see and hear everything. Turning so the drone couldn't see his gestures, he put a finger to his lips and stabbed a finger toward the robo bee.

He whispered, "To be continued."

Then something caught his attention. Off to the east, about a mile away, deep in a sheltered wing of the bay, a catamaran with the sleek lines of a Catana—a drop-dead magnificent boat—was just then gliding toward a sloop at anchor. He whipped out his binoculars. Yes. That was Dogu's catamaran *Bora*, and the sloop was named the *Profit*. Who did Sophia say was the captain? Abdul. Abdul Husseini.

Giving up on any thought of a romantic lunch, Adam keyed his mic, described the boats' location, and said, "Sophia, can you get some drones over there? Dogu is meeting up with *Profit*."

"I'm on it. Already got 'em close by."

Adam and Tripnee watched as the drone that had been hovering near them shot off down the mountain toward the two boats.

"See what I mean?" Tripnee said. "She's spying on us."

"Hold on, there could be an innocent explanation," Adam said as he studied the two terrorist's boats through his binoculars. "Maybe she had one positioned near us to be ready for this sort of situation? Or maybe she's just a little jealous?"

"Wake *up*. I'm telling you, the woman's poison."

"Well, at the moment she seems to be a solid agent with one hell of a skill set crucial to our mission."

"Blind asshole."

"Look, we've got to hold our team together. The consequences of failure are unthinkable. Unthinkable. So, hold it together."

Her eyes wild, Tripnee clenched her jaw.

Adam put an arm around her and his face softened. "We'll keep an eye on her, okay? But we've got to track down every single one of those goddamn nukes, and we need her to do it."

Tripnee's jaw trembled while her chest convulsed, rapidly rising and falling. Was she hyperventilating? Was she okay?

Adam reeled inside. Not only was he worried about Tripnee, he had a strange foreboding about what was about to go down aboard the terrorist's boats. As he watched through his long lenses, *Bora* came to rest alongside the anchored *Profit*, *Bora's* crew went aboard the other boat, and then both crews went below decks.

Perhaps to calm herself, or perhaps because her brain was always in overdrive, Tripnee got out her own binoculars. She read aloud the name written big across the transom of the second boat, "*Profit.*" Then she said, "Ha. Get it? A clever way to hide a reference to Prophet Muhammad in plain sight, especially from English speakers."

Sophia's voice crackled over their earpieces. "Drones are aboard. Patching the audio through to you now."

Dogu's voice, then others, yelled, "*Assalamu alaikum!*"

After shouts of "Die, traitors!" Adam and Tripnee's earpieces reverberated with the deafening rata-tat-tat of AK-47s mixed with prolonged, blood-curdling screaming. Suddenly, all was quiet.

Then they heard a voice: "Dogu, how could you?"

Dogu said, "*MashaAllah.*"

"We've known each other for years. Why? Why? *Why?*"

"I listen. I pay attention. You let it slip. You don't like our plan. The fact is, you cannot be trusted. So, you die. Allah willed it."

"But Dogu, I'm begging you. You and I grew up together. We are brothers fighting for Allah."

"I know you too well, brother Galen. You would report everything to Cyclops. Cyclops must never learn of our secret meeting, of our plans—and especially of me and my crew killing you. Allah commands."

"You always had the hot blood, Dogu. Hot blood does not win wars. Cool heads, like Cyclops, win wars. Thinking ahead smart, like Cyclops, wins wars."

Because only she could see the video feed coming from the drone, Sophia narrated, her voice tense, "Dogu is putting a knife to Galen's throat."

Then over their earpieces Adam and Tripnee heard Galen cry out, "Have you lost your mind? Cyclops even now sees what you do. May Allah take you down."

An ear-piercing scream was cut short, then there was gurgling.

"*Allahu Akbar.*"

Silence.

Sophia gasped. "Dogu slit Galen's throat. The dirty, dirty rotten bastard."

As Sophia narrated, Adam and Tripnee's earbuds filled with the sounds of Dogu and his crew searching every inch of *Profit.* Eventually, they found a suitcase nuke and several duffle bags of money. Curiously, instead of carrying these aboard their boat *Bora,* they stuffed them back into their hiding places on *Profit.*

Seen from high up the mountain, the two terrorists' boats appeared for all the world like a perfect picture of idyllic elegance and beauty, giving no hint of the horrors within. But the bloody reality sent Adam and Tripnee hauling ass down the mountain back to *Dream Voyager*. Nuclear bombs in the hands of murderous fanatics were on boats anchored a mile away.

CHAPTER 13

NAOUSA MARINA

As Adam and Tripnee sprinted along the quay, a cutter-rigged yawl jockeyed for position in the constricted harbor. Suddenly, the yawl dropped anchor and, angling across the violent, gusting *meltemi*, came flying stern first right into the tight slot between *Dream Voyager* and the next boat over.

The yawl had its fenders out; its crew stood ready with more hand-held fenders; and Adam and Tripnee hurried aboard *Dream Voyager* to assist with fenders of their own.

As the yawl's stern neared the quay, its crew made the classic newbie error of attempting to throw their entire stern-line coils. Super heavy, these dropped straight into the water, where they were sucked down toward the boat's reversing propeller, threatening to disable the boat. The skinny, intense skipper screamed profanities at his crew, adding to the mayhem.

At the last possible moment, the wild-eyed captain narrowly avoided catastrophe by finally throwing his transmission into forward. This pushed the submerged lines away from his prop, and sent his boat scooting back out into the small, windswept harbor. He then reset his anchor and jockeyed into position for a second try, which also failed because crew and captain repeated their same mistakes.

Adam didn't need this. He had to get *Dream Voyager* underway to go after Dogu. But he couldn't pull out while the big yawl thrashed back and forth, repeatedly backing in and accelerating out right next to them.

On the third frantic attempt, Adam and Tripnee yelled instructions to the yawl's traumatized crew and got in position themselves on the quay to receive the tossed lines. This time the yawl, which had the name *Humbaba* emblazoned across its stern, finally got its lines ashore and completed its mooring.

When Tripnee and Adam descended into *Dream Voyager's* salon, they found Sophia still diligently monitoring Dogu. They cooked up an assault plan, and the three of them went on deck to get underway only to find that a second boat, a sleek 70-foot schooner named *Dido*, was backing into the open slot on their starboard, windward side.

Dido was crewed by what looked like fourteen or so olive-skinned, well-oiled nineteen-to-twenty-two-year-old men in thong Speedos. Instead of using hand-held fenders, these muscular young men threw their massed bodies—like the Iwo Jima flag raisers but more compressed together—into the task of keeping their upwind boat from grinding against *Dream Voyager*.

Adam dropped a two-foot-diameter fender between the two boats, and—lucky thing—for it was squeezed down to a thin pancake as *Dido* jammed in to complete her Med-mooring.

Finally, they could get underway.

But Sophia stepped in close to Adam, and whispered, "I don't believe it. We've got to talk. Below."

Sophia led the way down into the salon where she slammed shut all the portholes and closed every curtain. Then she turned to Adam and Tripnee. "It's impossible. It just can't happen, but the fact is these two new boats next to us are crewed by Cyclops' men."

"Are you nuts?" Tripnee exclaimed. "Now you think every boat in the Greek islands is crewed by terrorists?"

"I know it defies logic," Sophia replied. "I'm not saying it's every boat. But the captains of these two new boats on either side of us are in the Interpol database. They're known IRGC operatives, and it's a good bet their crews are as well."

"Are you sure?" Adam asked.

"The captain of the boat on our starboard side—"

"*Dido*," Adam supplied.

"...is Ismail Kazmi," Sophia said. "The guy's a known terrorist. And so is the captain of the other boat—"

"*Humbaba*," Adam offered.

"...Yeah, *Humbaba*. That captain is Abd Quddus, a big-time terrorist linked to the attack on the Charlie Hebdo cartoonists in Paris."

"Well, *Humbaba* is an odd name," Tripnee commented. "In what's considered the first work of Western literature, Gilgamesh fights the monster Humbaba. If Gilgamesh represents Western civilization, Humbaba represents mythical, god-like forces that challenge the West."

"Yes," Sophia added, "and Gilgamesh is attacked because Humbaba's job is to protect a sacred forest. So, in Islamic eyes, Humbaba could be seen as protecting the sacred, the pure, the natural, the way things are truly meant to be."

Tripnee nodded slowly. "That's right."

"Interesting," Adam said. "Let's stay put long enough to figure out if these boats have nukes. But at the same time, Sophia, we need you to monitor Dogu and make sure his two nukes don't get away."

CHAPTER 14
CYCLOPS: TAQIYYA

P raise be to Allah.

"Taqiyya sanctions dissimulation, deception, lying. We are commanded to do whatever it takes, including lying, to destroy our enemies and spread Islam. The most perfect human, Prophet Muhammad, made this abundantly clear. *Taqiyya* is Islamic warfare." —Cyclops

Tafsir on Qur'an Surah 3:28: "Al-Bukhari recorded that Abu Ad-Darda' said, 'We smile in the face of some people although our hearts curse them.' Al-Bukhari said that Al-Hasan said, 'The *Tuqyah* is allowed until the Day of Resurrection. Allah said.'"

"If you (Muslims) are under their (non-Muslim) authority, fearing for yourselves, behave loyally to them with your tongue while harboring animosity for them...." —Muhammad ibn Jarir at-Tabiri, Jami' al-Bayan 'an ta'wil ayi'l-Qur'an al-Ma'ruf: Tafsir at-Tabari, explaining Qur'an Surah 3:28.

"If you fear treachery from any of your allies, you may fairly retaliate by breaking off your treaty with them."—Qur'an Surah 8:51.

In his court proceedings, 9/11 jihad hero Kalid Sheikh

Muhammad gloriously gave voice to Prophet Muhammad's deep truth: "War is deceit."

Bismillah. In the name of Allah.

CHAPTER 15

DIDO AND HUMBABA

Sophia set to work with her drones. At the same time, Adam and Tripnee did their own sleuthing.

Tripnee, her golden skin glowing in a pink bikini, stretched out on *Dream Voyager*'s starboard foredeck while half of *Dido*'s young all-male crew drooled over their ship's rail a few feet away.

One crew member in a Speedo with no more fabric than a jock strap, took a long, slow hose shower nearby. Soaping and rinsing himself again and again, he repeatedly lifted the tiny Speedo away from his groin to allow the water to flow more freely, all the while his eyes going frequently to Tripnee, and, when she glanced his way, flashing a beckoning smile.

"Are you on a charter? Where are you headed?" she asked, her luxuriant, shoulder-length, raven hair dancing in the breeze.

"Never mind that," the extremely well-built young man said, who was a head taller than his companions. "I'm Kurt Latifi. How about you and me go for stroll?"

"Join us for a party," another said.

Meanwhile, near the stern, Adam struck up a conversation with the intense, sinewy captain on their port side, Abd Quddus. Adam asked about the boat name *Humbaba*.

"*Humbaba*," Quddus said, "was a character in Gilgamesh. The first great book of Western literature."

"Yeah? You've studied Western literature?" Adam asked.

"Absolutely. The name honors Western literature and the great traditions of the West."

Adam raised his margarita, "To Western Civilization."

Quddus doffed his captain's hat, gave a little bow, then raised his own drink, "But of course, to Western Civilization."

"It looks like your crew is pretty green."

"No kidding. When it comes to sailing, they're buffoons."

"They chartered your boat?"

"No, no. I'm no charter captain. We're just friends on a lark. Sailing wherever."

The conversation ended when Quddus abruptly climbed out of sight down into his boat.

Later, the trio regrouped in the salon of *Dream Voyager.*

Grimacing, Tripnee mused, "Of course, actual terrorists would have a cover story. But if these guys are actual jihadis, either they've perfected great disguises or they're piss-poor terrorists."

"How so?" Adam asked.

"You'd expect, in some deluded way, for them to see themselves as devout warriors for Islam. But the *Dido* crew seems to be really and truly just a bunch of empty-headed kids looking to get laid."

"They're oddballs all right," Sophia said, "and most of them are not in the Interpol database. But they're definitely warriors. Get a load of this."

Adam and Tripnee gathered around Sophia's laptop which showed Captain Quddus sitting with both his crew and the *Dido* crew, apparently aboard *Humbaba.*

"Don't worry, they're clueless," Quddus said.

"The guy has no idea who we are?"

"That's Ismail Kazmi of *Dido,*" Sophia said.

"He's an ignorant American," Quddus said. "He doesn't even know who Gilgamesh was, let alone *Humbaba.*"

"He bought your cover story?" Kazmi asked.

"The guy's a pushover," Quddus answered. "Totally gullible."

"Still, it's important we practice and perfect our cover stories," Kazmi said, "so when we are put under scrutiny, we can go on fooling them."

"You're saying we should lie?" a new voice asked.

"That's the guy on *Dido* who invited me to take a stroll," Tripnee said, "Kurt Latifi."

"No, no," Kazmi said. "It's *taqiyya*. The Prophet is very clear. When talking to infidels, we are commanded to say whatever will spread Islam and advance the cause of Allah."

"Whether it is true or not?" Latifi asked.

"That is not the way to ask the question. The question is: What is the higher truth, the higher value?" Kazmi instructed him. "The higher truth, the highest value, is spreading the faith. Anything that hinders spreading Islam is a sin. Anything— *anything*—that spreads the faith is holy. *Anything*. That is *taqiyya*."

There was a hushed pause in the conversation aboard *Humbaba*, then Abd Quddus boomed, "Infidels are stupid and gullible. My question is: Did Allah intend for us to take so much joy in fooling them and killing them?"

Pointing to an object partially visible on the laptop screen, something poking out from a cubby in a far corner of *Humbaba*'s salon, Adam said, "Sophia, can you zoom in on this?"

A movement of her virtual controls adjusted the drone's optics and brought the object into sharp focus: A suitcase nuke.

CHAPTER 16

THE PARTY

"We're surrounded. Nineteen of them. Three of us. How in hell are we going to take down so many?"

Got to think outside the box.

Sophia outlined just such an idea. Adam was impressed. It was outside the box all right. And for that very reason just might work. Diabolical as hell. Fight evil with the devil's own tools. Just don't ever get on this woman's bad side.

"Gotta love arsenic. Colorless, odorless, tasteless. Deliciously lethal." Sophia flashed an evil smile, coming out of her cabin with a small backpack. She reached in and pulled out a sealed canister the size of a loaf of bread. "This special formulation is slow to act, but when it does, it knocks 'em dead fast."

"Horrendous but clever," admitted Tripnee. "Used since Roman times to off relatives and rivals."

"What about us?" Adam asked. "How are we going to keep from getting poisoned?"

"Got us covered two ways." Sophia lifted a pitcher from her pack. "See this? When you press this button inside the handle, it pours from a hidden chamber. That'll be how we pour drinks for the three of us. For our guests, we'll pour from the main chamber, which we'll refill from the big, refreshing, arsenic-laden, knock 'em dead Mojito punch bowl."

"And the other way we're protected?" Tripnee asked.

"My homeopathic antidote." Sophia held up a screw-top plastic bottle the size of a hand grenade. "We each need to take three doses of this before our party, just in case."

Tiny bikinis did the trick. Tripnee invited the *Dido* crew to a party on the *Voyager*, while Sophia, in a minuscule number little bigger than three eye patches, went aboard *Humbaba* to welcome that contingent, and all accepted. Pretty soon, both terrorist crews came swaggering aboard.

Adam figured his best move was to keep a low profile and appear drunk. To downplay his height and physique, he slouched in a back corner of the cockpit hunched over in loose, shabby clothes. To conceal any alpha-male vibe, he took on a deer-in-the-headlights look and pretty much continuously smiled and bobbed his head. To subtly encourage drinking, but without overdoing it, he acted more and more drunk and oblivious as he chugged what looked like Mojito after Mojito, nevertheless on alert and ready for action all the while, beneath the bowing and scraping.

Tripnee and Sophia poured drinks, chatted up the guests, poured more drinks, laughed, smiled, playfully swatted away grabby hands while pouring more and more drinks. The *Dido* and *Humbaba* crews seemed to be swallowing the charade hook, line, and sinker. Beautiful.

Well, except for three guys.

Kurt Latifi, stronger and taller than the others, stood apart on *Dream Voyager*'s stern deck. Glowering, he observed the proceedings without taking part.

Not good.

And Ismail Kazmi and Abd Quddus talked quietly on the bow, with no drinks in hand. Even worse.

Sophia made her way around, offering mojitos to these holdouts several times, but each time they refused. Seeing the problem, Tripnee approached Kurt with a big drink in each hand.

Coquettishly brushing her hip across the front of his tiny Speedo, she said, "Maybe later, after a few drinks, we can take that stroll."

Kurt's eyes lit up. "Forget the drinks, let's go."

"No drinks, no stroll."

The man grabbed her wrists, making her drop the glasses, and pulled her toward him. She brought a knee up into his groin with enough force to make him release her arms, but not enough to double him over or draw attention.

"Bitch."

Smiling, Tripnee touched a finger to the man's lips and spread her other hand on his chest. "Now, now. You're a strong, clever man. I like you and I'd love to take that stroll. But you're going to have to act like a gentleman."

Apparently amazed and won over by Tripnee's aplomb—and touch—and promise of bliss to come, Kurt actually nodded.

Adam had leapt to his feet and started toward them at the beginning of this interaction, when Kurt had seized Tripnee's wrists. But when Tripnee somehow quickly charmed and mollified the guy, Adam sat back down.

"So," Tripnee whispered to Kurt, "we're going to walk over to the others and socialize and have a few drinks."

"And the stroll?"

"Later," she said with a wink.

As Tripnee and Kurt walked past his vantage point at the stern end of the cockpit, Adam took this in. *Okay, progress.* But the two guys on the bow were going to be trouble.

The gathering picked up energy. Buzzed with alcohol but not yet feeling the arsenic, the men began refilling their drinks directly from the virulent Mojito bowl. Grabby hands reached with increasing force and frequency for Sophia and Tripnee, but these capable women held their own with deft blocks and parries. Interestingly, Kurt now apparently felt a possessory interest. Being bigger, stronger and something of a natural leader, he, with an occasional word or look and with a few solid punches, helped keep his companions in check and maintain a certain outward decorum. At least enough for Adam to disappear down the companionway.

Alone in *Dream Voyager*'s salon, Adam checked the Glock pistol with silencer jammed into his belt at the small of his back. Satisfied, he crept toward the bow. He eased himself onto an upper bunk in the forward-most cabin directly below a partially open ventilation hatch. Controlling his breathing, careful to make absolutely no sound, he listened to the conversation on the deck above.

A voice said quietly in Arabic, "Can you believe this Adam guy?" It was *Dido*'s captain, Ismail Kazmi.

Humbaba's captain, Abd Quddus, replied, "The guy's an infidel *kafir* asshole. A complete fool."

"I wonder."

"He's back there somewhere sitting on his ass getting drunk while his women throw themselves at our men."

"But is he really drunk?" Kazmi asked. "A while ago I saw him jump up, looking damned alert."

"Yeah, I saw that, too. But he plopped right back down when the booze hit him."

"I don't know. Something about the guy, and the women, too, worries me."

"How so?"

"Something's not right. It's like they just want to get us all drunk."

"To what end? To rob us? There're too many of us."

"I dunno. I smell a rat. It's a weird party."

"Maybe," Quddus said, "you're so deep into *taqiyya* and

deception, you think everyone is lying and up to no good."

"You know, brother, everyone is up to no good."

"You worry too much," Quddus said. "They're typical decadent Americans. It's an infidel party."

"You don't think they know something?"

"These people know nothing, suspect nothing. They're way too stupid. I've seen it a hundred times. This right here is the decadent West. It's why Islam will triumph."

"If the Great Satan is so stupid," Kazmi asked, "why are our men drooling over those women? Our men are thinking with their cocks."

"Don't worry. These women are *kafirs*, infidels. They don't matter. And the men are learning how to mingle with Americans and practice the cover story."

"I'm telling you something's just not right. I'll bet if I search this boat, we'll find that these aren't just typical decadent Westerners."

At that moment, fingers grasped the hatch lid inches above Adam's head. Adam barely had time to slide down and tuck into the lower bunk.

Kazmi dropped through the hatch onto the upper bunk, then slid off it. As his feet hit the deck, Adam clamped a hand over his mouth and with a swift rotation of the neck killed the guy.

Quddus' face appeared in the hatchway above. As the man's vision adjusted to the near total darkness of the cabin, his eyes popped wide. The instant he opened his mouth to yell, Adam brought up his silenced pistol and put a bullet between his eyes. *Psst.* Reaching up, Adam pulled Quddus's limp body down through the opening.

As he started to reach up again to close the hatch, footsteps came near on the deck above. A slurred voice said in Arabic, "Where'd they go? They were here a minute ago."

Adam quickly stuffed both bodies out of sight deep into the

lower bunk and covered them with a blanket. Then, holding his Glock behind his back, he yelled up through the still open hatchway, "Welcome. Come on down and join the party."

A face appeared in the opening. "Some party. Where're Kazmi and Quddus?"

Just as Adam was about to bring his Glock around to plug this third guy, hard steel jammed into the back of his neck.

"Stinking infidel."

Adam's gun was ripped from his grasp. Turning, he looked into the barrel of a large-caliber pistol inches from his left eye. With his other hand, the sweaty terrorist aimed the Glock at Adam's right eye.

"What is this?" Adam asked. "You don't like the party?"

Coming down through the hatch, the other guy aimed a third pistol at Adam's head.

"What were you going to do with this gun?"

Both men dripped sweat and slurred their words, but showed no signs of passing out. When was the damned arsenic going to kick in?

"I heard something up on the bow," Adam said. "Thought it might be prowlers, thieves."

Neither gunman looked under the blanket on the lower bunk. The instant they did, Adam was done for.

"What happened to Kazmi and Quddus?"

"How would I know? They're your captains."

Noticing the bunk, one of the terrorists said, "What's this?" and reached for the blanket.

For a moment, both looked toward the bunk, and that split second was all Adam needed. In one smooth blur of motion, he knocked the three pistols up, seizing them in the same instant. Two in his right hand, the third in his left. Wrenching the weapons free, he dislocated three trigger fingers in the process. Unfortunately, two of the guns went off in the process, emitting loud bangs and sending slugs into the underdeck. Getting his hand onto the grip of his Glock, he put a bullet into the head of each of his guests. *Psst, psst.* Then, less than a second later, he tapped each noggin again. *Psst, psst.*

Fifteen more terrorists aboard, all headed his way. He closed and locked the hatch, and tucked into a corner where he could pick off attackers as they came through the narrow cabin door one-by-one.

He didn't have to wait long. In less than a minute, one, two, three terrorists entered, and Adam dropped each with a bullet to the head. *Psst, psst, psst.*

No more came through. Seeing the first three cut down no doubt gave the others pause. Adam moved to see up the passageway. Men were backing away. He raised his weapon, but realized they weren't backing way, but were collapsing backward, forward, in all directions. The arsenic had finally kicked in. It was about bloody fucking time.

.

CHAPTER 17

PROFIT

His eyes alight, Adam outlined a plan to his team. Nodding with approval, they leapt into action, starting the engines and casting off the mooring lines of all three sailboats. With Adam leading on *Dido*, Tripnee next on *Humbaba*, and Sophia bringing up the rear on *Dream Voyager*, they raised anchors and slipped out of Naousa Harbor.

As soon as they were lost in the night out of sight from the marina, they rafted the boats together and thoroughly searched *Dido* and *Humbaba*. On each, as expected, they discovered a suitcase nuke, bags of U.S. currency, and caches of arms and ammo, which they stowed aboard *Dream Voyager*.

Then, as the three yachts jostled together in the fierce *meltemi*, they dragged the nineteen bodies below deck into the other two boats.

Adam and Tripnee strapped on bulletproof body armor, pulled on black tactical assault clothing, selected their weapons of choice for close-in combat, and made other preparations. Sophia checked her drones and reported *Bora* and *Profit* were still rafted together less than a mile away in Ormos Langeri, an anchorage on the east side of Naousa Bay. But there was activity aboard the two boats, which could mean one or both were preparing to depart.

Adam, Tripnee, and Sophia's three-boat fleet motored on across the broad bay with all lights out. Sophia, who had her laptops set up around the helm of *Dream Voyager*, reported over their earbud comms, "*Bora*'s on the move, but *Profit*'s staying put. Looks like Dogu's split his crew."

"How many aboard *Profit*?"

"I count four."

Adapting his plan on the fly, Adam announced, "We take out *Profit*, then chase *Bora*."

There, a quarter mile away, visible through night-vision goggles, *Profit* floated peacefully at anchor— all alone. Like a sitting duck.

Per the plan, Adam split to the right with *Dido*, Tripnee swung *Humbaba* left, and Sophia hung back on *Dream Voyager*. The goal was to eliminate *Profit*'s crew, recover any nukes, sink *Profit*, *Dido*, and *Humbaba*, and be long gone before the boats or bodies were discovered. So far, so good. *Dido* and *Humbaba*'s engines were running smooth, throttles wide open. The two boats accelerated to maximum hull speed. Circling, they converged on *Profit*—*Dido* speeding in from the east and *Humbaba* from the west. Yes! The timing looked good. Adam and Tripnee would burst out of the night and simultaneously crash into *Profit*. A nice little surprise for its terrorist crew.

But something was wrong. Muzzle flashes. AK-47 machine gun fire erupted from *Profit*. Bullets raked *Dido*'s hull and tore through its windscreen.

"*Humbaba*'s taking fire!" Tripnee shouted.

"Break off, Tripnee! Break off!" Adam yelled into his comm. "Let me do this one. Something alerted these guys. Stay back. Pick 'em off from a safe distance."

"To heck with that," Tripnee argued back. "I'm going in, too."

Typical Tripnee. No common sense. Well, thank God he'd anticipated a fire fight and had hauled up and braced a heavy salon table top in front of each ship's wheel on his and Tripnee's boats.

Now, an incoming hailstorm of lead ripped into the thick slab of mahogany inches in front of Adam's face. The wood jumped and shook with the ongoing ratta-tat-tat pounding—but so far it was stopping the bullets. Adam prayed that Tripnee's tabletop was doing the same.

Dido and *Humbaba* closed on *Profit* from opposite directions. Blasting away, the AK-47s reached a frantic crescendo. Then, double whammy. The sharp bow stem of Adam's *Dido* sliced right across *Profit*'s center cockpit, silencing, at least for the moment, the three guns firing from there. *Humbaba*, artfully guided by Tripnee, plowed across *Profit*'s forward deck straight into the forward hatch, instantly crushing the fourth shooter.

With a Glock 19 in each hand, Adam peered over his barricade. A terrorist had popped up and was drawing a bead on Tripnee, his head exposed. Adam put two slugs into the guy's right ear.

"Who knows, might improve his hearing?"

Not sure about the remaining terrorists, but taking no chances, Adam tucked his pistols into their holsters, and pulled a grenade from a leg pouch, pulled the pin on the grenade, counted the seconds to allow the least amount of time for the terrorists to throw it back, then tossed it at the *Profit*'s cockpit, expecting it to explode on impact. But, son of a gun, one of the terrorists, reacting like an expert baseball player, took his AK-47 by the barrel—despite the fact it had to be red hot—and used the weapon like a bat to knock the pineapple back toward Adam.

Adam dove behind his tabletop in the nick of time.

KA-BLAM. That was close. The mahogany slab had held, but just barely. In places, he could now see right through it.

He saw two terrorists when he peered through the cracks.

Realizing the splintered table top was on its last legs, they were bringing up their weapons and in moments would blast the weakened table to smithereens, and in the process turn him into a bloody pulp.

Pop. Pop. Silence.

"It's okay," Tripnee said. "They're dead."

The collisions had ripped open the hulls of the terrorists' sailboats, and all three were going down. Fast. After Tripnee came over from *Humbaba*, they both took off their body armor, and climbed down *Profit*'s companionway. The water was at knee level and rising. Adam went forward, while Tripnee worked sternward. Ripping open cabinets and closets, and submerging to lift up deck boards, they searched and searched, but found only money.

Adam dove down in chest-deep water in *Profit*'s bow cabin now under *Humbaba*'s pulverized intruding bow, and struggled to lift deck boards. The floor panels were wedged tight, probably because the boat's entire bow and hull had been distorted by the collisions.

Finally, with his lungs screaming, in one final desperate attempt, drawing on his utter last reserves, he gave a mighty heave and the boards came free. There it was. A suitcase nuke, looking like it was still intact in its waterproof case.

Grabbing the bomb, Adam tried to rise up to get a breath. But the sea filled the small cabin clear to the ceiling. Lungs screeching in agony, gripping the nuke, he dove back under *Humbaba*'s bow, and kicked, swam, crawled underwater back toward the companionway. Tripnee appeared when he was halfway and everything was going black. Blessed, amazing woman, she pressed her mouth to his and breathed into him a lungful of the most ethereal, delicious air any human had ever received.

Together they swam for the companionway. At the surface,

amazingly, Adam found he still held the nuke and Tripnee had two duffle bags, which turned out to be filled with hundred-dollar bills. The top of *Profit*'s cabin was underwater and sinking fast. *Dido*, *Humbaba*, *Profit* and a bunch of dead terrorists were going down. Sophia backed *Dream Voyager*'s sugar-scoop stern to within a few feet and, grabbing up their weapons, armor, the duffles, and nukes, Adam and Tripnee scrambled aboard.

CHAPTER 18

CYCLOPS: APOSTASY

“The Messenger of Allah said, “If someone changes his religion—then strike off his head.” —al-Muwatta of Imam Malik (36.18.15)

“When a person who has reached puberty and is sane, voluntarily apostatizes from Islam, he deserves to be killed.” — *Reliance of the Traveller* (Handbook of Islamic Law) o8.1. (o8.4 affirms that there is no penalty for killing an apostate). Sahih Bukhari (52:260). “…The Prophet said, ‘If somebody (a Muslim) discards his religion, kill him.’”

There is a consensus by all four schools of Sunni Islamic jurisprudence (Maliki, Hanbali, Hanafi, and Shafi), as well as classical Shiite jurists, that apostates from Islam must be put to death. —Cyclops

As Abu Bakr, Muhammad’s closest companion, explained in a letter at the time, his Prophet “struck whoever turned his back to him until he came to Islam, willingly or grudgingly.” Thus did Abu Bakr promise to “burn them with fire, slaughter them by any means, and take women and children captive” any who left Islam. —Hadith, al-Tabari, v10 p.55-57.

“Ali, the fourth ‘Rightly Guided Caliph’ was Muhammad’s

son-in-law and one of the first converts to Islam. He had people burned alive for wanting to leave Islam." Hadith—al-Tabari, v.17 p.191.

"All systems of Islamic law have prescribed the death penalty for Muslims choosing to leave Islam for 1400 years." The popular Muslim scholar, Zakir Naik, affirming in 2013 that the death penalty should be applied to those who leave Islam, on British television on the Peace TV channel.

"Apostasy from Islam… is a crime punishable by death. The Prophet (peace be upon him) limited capital punishment to these three crimes only, saying: 'The shedding of the blood of a Muslim is not lawful except for one of three reasons: a life for a life, a married person who commits *zina* (adultery), and one who turns aside from his religion and abandons the community.'"— Islamic scholar Sheikh Yusuf al-Qaradawi, head of the European Council for Fatwa and Research, and president of the International Union for Muslim Scholars, *The Lawful and the Prohibited in Islam*, 1960.

"In any case, the heart of the matter is that children born of Muslim lineage will be considered Muslims and according to Islamic law, the door of apostasy will never be opened to them. If anyone of them renounces Islam, he will be as deserving of execution as the person who has renounced *kufr* [disbelief] to become a Muslim, and again has chosen the way of *kufr*. All the jurists of Islam agree with this decision. On this topic absolutely no difference exists among the experts of *shari'ah*. —Abul Ala Mawdudi, founder of Jamaat-e-Islami party, *The Punishment of the Apostate According to Islamic Law*, 1994.

"Apostates from Islam can be murdered freely and legally… this… is necessary."—Dr. Wafa Sultan, *A God Who Hates*, 2011.

"Anyone who turns their back on Islam must be executed. This is confirmed by the words and deeds of Muhammad."—Cyclops

CHAPTER 19

THE WIDE AEGEAN

Dogu Kubilay's Catana catamaran, *Bora,* raced south with *Dream Voyager* in hot pursuit.

Sophia looked up from her drone-tracking screen. "*Bora*'s going between the islands of Antiparos and Paros. Maybe headed for Folegandros."

The *meltemi* subsided to a dead calm and the cobalt-blue waters of the Aegean went from rough to choppy to glassy. Switching from sail to motor power, they did their best to stay within drone transmission range of *Bora*, but whether under sail or motor power, the catamaran was lighter and faster. How does a slower boat catch a lighter, faster boat?

"Listen to this." Sophia put the drone's audio feed over *Dream Voyager*'s speakers:

"Dogu, a change of plan."

Adam recognized the voice. "That's Roxanna."

"Rasheed Houssein and his crew just anchored off Santorini. You know what must be done."

"Rasheed," Dogu said. "Doing Galen was bad enough. But Rasheed's married to my sister."

Roxanna's voice had a steely edge: "Galen was sure to betray us. Rasheed is a different case altogether. The fool renounced Islam! He was found guilty of apostasy in a Shari'a court and a fatwa was issued. The man must die, and you are our enforcer."

She paused, seeming to expect agreement, but Dogu said,

"There must be another way."

Roxanna said, "Get a grip on yourself, Dogu. You're my rock. Rasheed is a convicted apostate who questions and doubts Allah."

"Rasheed is family. My sister Fatima loves him, needs him. Fatima's children, my nephews, need him."

"These are harsh times—but also glorious. The Prophet's companions sacrificed family and friends for the faith. *Inshallah*, you must do the same."

There was a long silence, then Dogu wept.

"Your deeds bring you and your crew closer to Allah. Be resolute. *Inshallah*, soon we will achieve greatness."

"*Allahu Akbar.*" More sobbing.

"*Allahu Akbar.* After Santorini, take care of things on Folegandros."

"I know. I know, Vathi Bay."

"Dogu's starting to crack," Adam said, "but he's going to take out another terrorist crew."

"Can you believe it? Killing his own brother-in-law for his religion," Tripnee said. "But it makes our job that much easier."

Sophia just scowled. Her screen showed Dogu changing course, heading southeast toward Santorini.

Instead of following, Adam cut the engine, and *Dream Voyager* slowed to a complete stop in the dead calm. Death and mayhem were afoot. But looking around, he saw only serene beauty. They floated in the heart of the Cyclades Islands. If north was twelve o'clock, encircling them, in clear view on the horizon, were Antiparos at one o'clock, Paros at two o'clock, Ios—the party island—at four, Sikinos at five, Folegandros at seven, the combined mass of Milos, Poliegos and Kimolos at nine, and Sifnos at ten. In this strategic central location, Adam, Tripnee, and Sophia could drift and listen in to see if the weeping Dogu would actually kill his own brother-in-law on

Santorini. Then they'd race to Folegandros to lie in wait, see who showed up—and hopefully collect their nukes.

While Dogu closed on Santorini, the three of them dove off the stern steps and swam in the warm, seemingly bottomless, cobalt-blue Aegean—and waited.

Eventually, Sophia, back at her computer, yelled, "It's happening. Dogu's talking to a skipper anchored at Santorini."

"…but you are killing your own people."

"That's got to be the brother-in-law, Rasheed Houssein," Sophia said.

Dogu said, "The holy book is clear: apostates—unbelievers, doubters, and waverers—must die. And you have been judged."

"But we are family. And who doesn't sometimes waver and question?"

"You forget. Apostasy, questioning, doubting Allah and Mohammad are sins punishable by death. You have been judged." He seemed to say it to strengthen his resolve.

"Dogu, I am on my knees before you. Think of my wife, your sister, Fatima. Think of our three boys, your nephews: Mohammad, Ammad, and little Rasheed named after you."

"*Allahu Akbar!*"

A scream. Then silence. Then quiet weeping, and the names, "Fatima, Mohammad, Ammad, Rasheed," repeated over and over.

CHAPTER 20

FOLEGANDROS

A dam fired up the engine, turned the bow toward Folegandros, and thrust the throttle full forward. Just then a small plane approached from the direction of Paros, circled overhead, then flew off—toward Folegandros. Adam's uplifted eyes followed the dot in the sky.

Something about that's not good.

Sitting at the nav desk, Adam opened his *Greek Waters Pilot* and studied the maps and write-up covering Folegandros. Two-miles wide and eight-miles long, the island was an arid, steep-sided ridge jutting some 1700 feet up out of the Aegean. A single road ran along the mountainous spine of the island, with a few spur roads and hiking trails extending down to bays and beaches. A number of settlements dotted the landscape here and there, but the only town of any size—Chora—was perched high on the island's central ridge.

Dogu was going to Vathi Bay on the island's southwestern side, so it was best not anchor there. But the sheltered harbor of Karavostassi near the eastern end, looked good for what Adam had in mind. They dropped anchor there in crystalline water, late in the afternoon.

Adam and Tripnee packed comm gear, night-vision scopes, weapons, body armor, and a few handy extras in fanny packs, glided ashore in the skiff, and found one of the islands' few taxis to take them up to Chora. Sophia remained aboard, her drones fanning out to surveil the island.

Chora turned out to be an ancient mountaintop fortress dating back to the middle ages. Its shady, oasis-like squares overflowed with old-world charm and invited exploration, but time was short. Dogu would soon enter nearby Vathi Bay, and they had to get into position beforehand. A trail on the outskirts of Chora led to a vantage point overlooking most of central Folegandros, including Vathi Bay. As the sun sank in the west, they paid off the taxi and set out along a wide, well-maintained path. An hour later, in darkening twilight, they arrived at the overlook.

They were just in time. There, far below, their night scopes revealed Dogu's *Bora* knifing through dark, glassy water, penetrating deep into the bay. The catamaran dropped anchor just off the small settlement of Agali, at the head of the bay. Wasting no time, Dogu climbed into a dinghy and motored toward shore. A car waiting in the dark on the outskirts of Agali flashed its lights. The terrorist pulled his boat up on the beach, jumped into the vehicle, and sped off. Adam and Tripnee had a clear view of his route, and watched as the vehicle climbed the winding road headed, apparently, toward Chora.

"Interesting," Adam said. "Dogu's the enforcer. He usually operates in force with his crew, but here he's going off alone. I wonder why?"

Tripnee stood solidly in a wide stance. "By my count, there should be three—or more—nukes on that boat. Let's go get 'em."

"Agreed," Adam said. Keying his earpiece, he filled Sophia in on the situation, and asked her to monitor Dogu while he and Tripnee dealt with *Bora*.

The trail was steep but wide and smooth as it switch-backed down to the shore of Vathi Bay. As they descended, they listened as Sophia's drones located and tracked Dogu's vehicle, which delivered the Islamist enforcer to a villa near Chora.

"Impressive," Sophia said. "The place has an infinity pool, floor-to-ceiling windows overlooking the Aegean, classic Greek charm like you can't believe."

"Who's there? Adam asked. "Who's Dogu meeting?"

"So far just one guy. I'll patch through the sound."

"Isa, you live well."

"Well, yes, old friend. Please do not tell Cyclops or Roxanna. They would not approve."

"True, they would not."

"What's wrong?"

"Why do you ask?"

"We've known each other how long?"

"Since we were children."

"Yes, forever. So, I know when you're troubled."

"It is forbidden to say anything."

"You're my dearest friend. Out with it."

Sophia interrupted, "My Interpol facial recognition software says this guy is Isa Kaan, captain of a sailboat named *Canan*. His boat's anchored right here in Karavostassi."

"Damn," Adam said. "Make sure the intruder alarms are on, and keep a weapon handy."

"Don't worry. Got that covered. Plus, I have sentry drones deployed." Sophia paused, then narrated the drone cam view on her computer screen: "Dogu is actually hunched over, sobbing."

Isa said, "It's okay, it's okay. You always had to be the strongest, the most devout. But I know you. I *know*. Deep down, you doubt. You waver. It's okay. We all do. It's only human."

Dogu wept. And wept. Then said, "Then you know. When I let myself think my own thoughts while reading the Qur'an, I found no answers. But I didn't know what to do, so I acted extra devout. Probably trying to convince myself. I fooled Roxanna, but not myself."

"I know."

"You know?"

"Yes, *habibi*, dear brother. And I know you were ordered to kill me here tonight."

"You know?"

"Believe me, dear friend. Being the enforcer would take its toll on anyone. But knowing you, I know it's killing you inside."

"I prayed every day. I took it seriously. I thought about what I believed."

"Yes, yes. You did. I saw it."

"I had to repress so many questions. The teachings were right, my doubts were wrong. I was wrong."

"You gave it your best effort. For years and years."

Adam and Tripnee reached the water's edge of Vathi Bay. Turning, they moved along the shoreline toward the village of Agali and the catamaran, *Bora*.

Dogu went on, "But so much is in clear conflict with what I, what anyone knows of good and bad."

"Believe me, brother. I know, I know."

"But what I am saying is, my words right now are punishable by death."

"Your only crime is thinking for yourself, using your brain."

Because only she could see the video, Sophia narrated, "Tears are pouring down the guy's face."

Dogu choked out, "But daring not to believe is a capital offense. I myself have often quoted Sahih Bukhari—'Kill those who change their religion.'"

"Yes," Isa said, "Mohammad said this many times. So, what does that tell you?"

Sobbing. "I don't know. I don't know." More sobbing. "How do you handle it?"

"I realized an obvious fact," Isa replied. "Not all Muslims think alike. It took time, but I gradually decided things don't have to be absolute, black or white."

"Apostasy?"

"To some, to absolutists. But not to me."

As they neared Agali, Adam and Tripnee found Dogu's skiff.

"Amazing," Adam said. "Sounds like the guy's ready to defect. But regardless, we've got to get those nukes."

"Amen to that."

With an easy coordination born of many dangerous adventures together, they readied their weapons and silently launched the dinghy. A former class-five river guide, Tripnee took the oars and soon had them gliding out in a wide circle around behind the big, dark catamaran. It looked like the crew was asleep with no sentry posted. But that would be tantamount to negligence. And the duo had learned that counting on your opponent's negligence was not conducive to survival.

Coming out of the night with the vast black Aegean behind them, they were, they hoped, hard to spot. After floating soundlessly up to an open ventilation port, Adam activated and dropped in one of his favorite devices, a canister of fast-acting sleeping gas, a mixture of sevoflurane, isoflurane, and halothane. Moving to the other side of the big cat, they dropped in another. Then, for good measure, they maneuvered to throw a third into the central cabin.

Bang. Bang. Bang. Gunshots rang out.

They threw themselves into the water, and surfaced in the protected airspace under the cabin between the cat's two hulls. Instinctively reaching for one another, they simultaneously asked in urgent whispers, "Are you okay?"

That was close. But thank God the shots missed. Probably fired off by a half-awake sentry.

Adam had lost the third canister, but fortunately his silenced

Glock was still in his waterproof fanny pack. Knowing the terrorists would expect intruders to climb aboard using the ship's stern steps, Adam swam to the bow and pulled himself up the anchor chain and pulled out his Glock as he crawled onto the catamaran's bow trampoline. Two figures, one towering, the other small, moved in the main cabin. Shooting through the boat's windshield, he dropped the big one with a bullet to the head. *Psst.*

Adam quickly swung his gun toward the smaller terrorist, but the guy was even quicker and ducked out of sight. Now exposed, Adam scrambled to the boat's starboard side to put a blank section of cabin wall between himself and the jihadi. Ratta-tat-tat. The terrorist opened up with what had to be an AK-47. Ratta-tat-tat. Bullets ripped straight through the cabin's fiberglass skin, searching for Adam. Ratta-tat-tat. Adam jumped sideways, but the pattern of puckering bullet holes came closer—and closer. Ratta-tat-tat-ratta-tat-tat.

Psst, psst. Tripnee's Beretta. Thump. The terrorist fell to the deck and the AK-47 went silent.

Sophia screamed over their headsets, "I've been shot!"

*   *   *

It turned out the other two members of *Bora*'s crew had been knocked out by the gas. Adam and Tripnee found them unconscious but alive in their bunks, and secured them with ankle and wrist cuffs. Figuring it was the fastest way to both secure the nukes and return to *Dream Voyager*, Adam and Tripnee fired up *Bora*'s engines, weighed anchor, and motored at full throttle out of Vathi Bay. Racing around the southern end of Folegandros, they entered Karavostassis and rafted *Bora* alongside *Dream Voyager*.

Sophia was badly bruised but alive. A black-clad assassin had somehow managed to creep aboard without triggering the alarms or sentry drones.

Adam frowned. "How in hell was that even possible?"

Fortunately, Sophia, who was after all a professional cop, had worn a Kevlar vest. The two bullets, delivered in quick double-tap assassin style, knocked her down and almost out. But she still had enough wits to play dead for a moment, then get off several shots. One or two of which apparently found their mark, because there was a trail of blood across the cockpit and down the stern steps. But they found no bodies floating in the vicinity or other traces of the attacker.

CHAPTER 21

MILOS

"There's news," Sophia said. "Big, terrible news. While you two were on Folegandros, just before the attacker came aboard, I decrypted a terrorist transmission. They know about *Dream Voyager*. That we're hunting them, taking them down one-by-one. But there's more. The boat captains are spooked. They're stepping up the attack schedule and rushing to depart for targets in Europe and America."

Adam's muscles tensed, his eyes narrowed. "We'll just have to pick up our pace. They've got to be stopped."

"And at the same fucking time," Tripnee said, "we've got to stay invisible."

"And make sure," Sophia added, "we're not being tracked."

"Also," Adam said, "we've got to be on guard. There's sure to be more attacks." Then, rising to his feet, he asked, "Do we know where any of these boats are?"

"I could only locate one so far," Sophia said, "a 118-foot, two-masted caique named *Helios*, on Milos."

"Forty miles west of here," Adam said.

"It's topping off provisions right now as we speak."

"We've got to move fast. But first we've got to deal with Isa Kaan's boat, *Canan*."

*   *   *

117

Adam and Tripnee strapped on rebreathers and eased below the surface on the far side of *Dream Voyager*, hopefully out of sight from prying eyes, including any with night-vision tech. Swimming side-by-side through the dark water, they crossed the harbor and surfaced at the bow of Isa Kaan's fifty-foot sloop *Canan*. Adam had a hunch, given its captain's apostasy—or awakening—that the crew would not be alert. It turned out, in fact, *Canan* was completely unguarded—and a search uncovered a nuke. Bringing up the anchor, they motored back over to *Bora* and *Dream Voyager*.

Still cloaked in the dark of night, Adam took the wheel of *Bora*, Tripnee stayed aboard *Canan,* and Sophia fired up *Dream Voyager*. One-by-one they motored the three boats out of Karavostassis, turned west to round the southern tip of Folegandros, and headed in the direction of Milos.

Once well out to sea, they rafted the three sailboats together. After stowing *Bora*'s two nukes and the one from *Canan* in the secret compartment deep in the belly of *Dream Voyager*, Adam and Tripnee brought the two surviving *Bora* crew members, a thin man and a muscular woman, aboard, checked to make sure they were immobilized in their bindings, and locked them in separate forward cabins.

Next, they activated timers on two incendiary grenades and tossed these into *Bora* and *Canan*. Then, as *Dream Voyager* accelerated away, self-igniting 4000-degree phosphorous explosions blasted the two terrorists' boats into towering columns of flame, which soon disappeared as the vessels sank beneath the waves.

"The next order of business," Adam said, "is to figure out how they found us."

Sophia, her back arched, held up a gadget the size of an iPhone. "Get a load of this baby. It detects listening bugs and hidden spy cameras."

While Sophia scanned *Dream Voyager* with her device, Tripnee physically searched every nook and cranny below deck, while Adam put on a powerful waterproof head lamp to search the ship's entire exterior above—and below—the waterline. He cut the engine and donned a rebreather for the underwater phase. Sophia and Tripnee came up empty, but Adam found a gizmo stuck to the hull deep underwater near the bow.

It turned out that the device, no bigger than a small iPad, sent out a long-range signal that was probably trackable all over the Aegean—and yet was so high-tech it evaded detection by Sophia's gadget. Adam strapped the device to a big beach ball with tape and webbing. According to the forecast, the *meltemi* would in the next couple of days go from zero to forty or fifty miles per hour. He dropped the ball overboard, fired up *Dream Voyager*, and accelerated west toward Milos. The three of them watched the ball as it faded into the distance. In a day or two it would be halfway to Africa, which should throw off whoever was tracking them, at least for a while.

Still riding an adrenaline rush, Adam, Tripnee, and Sophia huddled together in the cockpit. Maybe they were finally coming together as a team.

Adam asked, "What do you make of Dogu Kubilay's and Isa Kaan's change of heart? Will more of these terrorists wake up?"

"No chance," Sophia said. "Of course, there are all sorts of Muslims. But *Jamaat-e Aleimlaq* is hard core. It's made up of doctrinaire extremists in the same mold as Osama bin Laden. With them, there's no wavering, no compromise, no tolerance. Period. They sacrifice everything: their future, their families, their children. I've tracked this group for years, and I can't think of a more extreme example of total conviction."

"But look at all the drinking and carousing," Adam said, "and the two guys who were tempted by the gold. How is that hardcore Islamic extremism?"

"Most of that is just for show," Sophia said. "Believe me. These guys are serious." She paused. Her face took on a wistful, faraway look. One eye pinched shut, and her hands clenched into fists. "Jihadis from this network have performed dozens of suicide bombings. Think of that level of conviction. To do that knowing you're going to kill people—and get killed yourself in the process."

Adam shook his head. "I just can't wrap my head around that. How can anyone even condone, let alone do such a thing?"

Tripnee said, "Suicide bombers have streets and public squares named after them in the Palestinian territories. They're honored as heroes, celebrated far more than we celebrate our own founding fathers."

Adam again shook his head. "Mad, depraved, deprived."

Sophia said, "No. Lots of these Believers are educated and come from well-off families, including from Europe. Like Osama bin Laden and the 9/11 terrorists, these guys are responding to something bigger than themselves. They literally, absolutely believe they are doing the bidding of the one true, real, actual God of the universe: Allah."

Taking in the enormity and horror they faced, Adam felt exhausted. Hell, they were all sleep-deprived. After checking his maps, he outlined a plan for the coming day. Then, with Sophia offering to take the coming watch, he and Tripnee went below and plunged into something akin to the sleep of the dead, but, for him, alive with nightmares.

As the sun rose the next morning, Adam groggily stumbled up the companionway as Sophia guided *Dream Voyager* into a small bay.

"Voudhia?" he asked.

"Yep."

"Well done."

There was that smile so dazzling he had to look away.

They were near the far northeastern corner of Milos. Roughly 13-miles-long by 6-miles-wide, Milos, like Santorini, had an enormous bay, Ormos Milou, in its center. Once the caldera of an ancient volcano, Ormos Milou was the thriving, bustling heart of the island—and not a good place to be if you wanted to stay out of sight. The remote backwater inlet of Voudhia, on the other hand, was perfect. Sheltered from the coming *meltemi* gale and, even more importantly, from prying eyes, it was linked by road to every sizable port on the island.

Desperate to catch *Helios* before it vanished with its nuke, Adam roused Tripnee and the pair quickly filled their fanny packs with what they'd need.

Adam grinned to see Tripnee bring her Banshee MR-57 with its 10" silencer and a bunch of 20-round magazines. A mini version of the AR-15, the light, ultra-compact sniper rifle fired small, fast bullets—rounds that were extra lethal because once they hit flesh, they stayed inside the body and did not go out the back. If you have to fight terrorists, it was good to have an intrepid, if slightly crazy, sharpshooter girlfriend with a cute, 4.6 pound machine gun accurate to well over 200 yards. Hell, he'd seen her obliterate targets with it at 500-yards.

They rode the dinghy to shore, and hired a local to drive them to the island's biggest port, Adamas, on the big interior bay, Ormos Milou. Meanwhile, Sophia already had drones fanning out over the island in search of the Cyclopean caique *Helios*.

When their vehicle crested the mountainous ridge encircling Ormos Milou, both Tripnee and Adam gasped at the sight before them.

"Imagine the scale," Tripnee said, "of the volcanic eruption that created this vast bay."

"Incredible."

Sophia's voice crackled over the earpieces of their encrypted radios. "I knew it. *Helios* is loading in broad daylight right on the main quay in Adamas. It dwarfs the boats around it. You should be able to see it from where you are."

Sure enough, there far below them was what had to be the 118-foot caique Med-moored to a wide quay. A short time later in the town of Adamas, they paid off their driver and mingled into the Greek Med scene of fit, suntanned people promenading along the quay and feasting in open-air cafés fronting Ormos Milou. They started wandering out along the quay to get a close-up look at their quarry. Halfway to the boat, Adam suddenly spun around, putting his back toward *Helios*. Tripnee followed suit.

"Roxanna's on board."

Praying they hadn't been spotted, Adam and Tripnee moved away, knowing not to glance rearward, trying to melt into the crowd, but feeling like they had targets emblazoned on their backs.

They watched the stately two-masted caique from a busy café across the cobblestone boulevard from the quay, far enough away but still with a clear view. One man topped off fuel tanks from a diesel tank truck; a second man filled water tanks with a hose from the quay's water line; and two other men carried supplies from a truck over a stern gangplank onto the vessel. Soon the activity stopped. The hoses were rolled up, two of the men drove the trucks away, and the other two men boarded the boat and entered the cabin.

Sophia's voice again crackled in their ear pieces. "I haven't been able to fly any drones inside the cabin, but I do have a visual through a window."

Tripnee said, "It looks like they just finished loading and are leaving. I think we're too late."

"Hold on a minute," Sophia said. "They're arguing about something. I made out the words, 'one last drink.'"

Abruptly, eight people, six men and two women, poured out of *Helios'* cabin, streamed across its gangplank, and came sauntering off the quay. One of the women was Roxanna. Adam and Tripnee subtly dropped their gazes and turned away.

"That looks like their whole crew," Adam said. "They may still have a sentry on board, but this looks like the best opportunity we're going to get."

CHAPTER 22

HELIOS

Roxanna and her companions walked off the quay and moved east along the waterfront boulevard toward the center of Adamas, fading into the crowd. A subliminal alarm fired in Adam's psyche. What was wrong? Not sure, but he insisted Tripnee stay in the café as lookout while he alone checked out *Helios*. She had a fit, but eventually agreed.

Adam crossed the boulevard and walked out along the ancient stone quay. The 118-foot, two-masted caique *Helios* looked quiet with no one stirring, and the yachts on either side also seemed quiet. Too quiet?

Figuring what the hell, Adam stepped onto the gangplank and boarded *Helios* at the stern. An above-deck one-story cabin ran the full length of the hull, except for a stern cockpit. Still no one visible. Adam crossed the cockpit and put his hand on the cabin door handle. It was unlocked. Pulling his silenced Glock from his fanny pack, he stepped into the spacious salon and closed the door behind him. The room appeared empty.

A long mahogany table able to seat maybe fourteen people stretched the length of the space. Large windows lined the walls to port and starboard, while floor-to-ceiling lockers of lustrous dark hardwood lined the bulkheads fore and aft.

Out of nowhere, a gun barrel jammed into the small of Adam's back.

"Don't move."

"Hold it right there."

"Drop it."

In the blink of an eye, gun barrels jutted from lockers, doorways, and a floor hatch. All aimed straight at him. Uzis and AK-47s. Eight, ten, a dozen.

It wasn't going to be easy to get the drop on so many, but there had to be a way. There was just too much at stake. Then, visible through the salon windows, armed men streamed aboard from boats moored alongside. Twenty or so men. All looking at Adam. All armed. It was a trap. They'd been lying in wait.

"Drop it. Or die."

Adam lowered his pistol. A savage blow struck him on the back of the head and the world went black.

*   *   *

Adam opened his eyes. His skull throbbed. He was collapsed in a chair with arms bound behind him. Clothes gone, shoes removed. Looking around, he saw he was in a small, dimly-lit cabin, probably below the waterline, down in the belly of the caique. A figure stood before him. A long, ugly knife and big wire cutters moved into his field of vision.

"You can make this easy or hard." It was Roxanna.

"What?"

"You're going to tell me everything. How you're tracking us. Who you're working with." The blade moved back and forth inches from his face. "Where's your boat? Where are my bombs?"

The knife suddenly shot straight toward his face, its tip almost touching his right eye.

"You can talk now while you're still in one piece, or you can talk later when you have no fingers, no toes, no teeth, no eyes, no balls, no cock. You choose. One way or the other, you will talk."

Helping this terrorist was not an option. But getting cut to pieces sounded less than ideal. What in hell was he going to do?

"So, what'll it be?" she demanded. "Are you Mossad? CIA? Where's your boat? Where are my nukes?"

"Your biggest problem," Adam said, "is you've got moles."

"Moles? No way."

"How else could I know it was you who negotiated the deal for the nukes? It was you who sailed them down through the Bosporus? And it was you who got the gold to finance the whole jihad?"

Roxanna's eyes opened wide in surprise, then narrowed to angry slits, her face contorted. Was she taken aback, thrown off balance? Was she buying it?

"You've got me," Adam said. "You believe in what you're doing—I respect that. In fact, I envy you. Me, I'm just a very, very highly paid assassin."

Roxanna's face remained a picture of rage, but she nodded, smiling slightly.

"I'll make you a deal," Adam continued. "We exchange information. We go back and forth. I tell you something and in exchange you tell me something. And afterward, if you're satisfied, you let me walk."

No doubt the woman would kill him in a heartbeat once she'd extracted the information she sought. But this could work in his favor. She'd probably be more willing to open up thinking whatever she shared would die with him. The key was to let her think she was the smarter, superior person. But whatever he did, he had slow things down. Gain time to figure something out. Some way, any way to survive.

Roxanna's eyes moved up and down the length of his naked body.

"I have admit, it would be a terrible waste to slice you up," she said, lowering the knife. "Even strapped down, I have to admit, you've got what I call apex male energy."

"Yeah?"

"I'm surrounded by dim-bulb males, a few alphas, lots of betas, and some omegas. I use 'em all—everyone Allah sends—but sadly no apex males like you. Too bad you're an infidel."

Clearly, she was playing him with flattery, but that could work both ways. "I have to return the compliment. You're one hell of a woman."

Like any true Believer, this woman was probably convinced she knew the Truth with a capital "T." And no doubt she was certain she had no vanity nor prejudices—which made her all the more susceptible to his playing upon them. Also, it didn't hurt that on some animal level she felt his male vibe.

"In fact, you're amazing," he said. "I think you're Cyclops. If you're not, you should be."

She tried to hide it, but her eyes brightened. She seemed to eat it up. "It's odd. The truth is, I don't know who Cyclops is. I've never met him."

"As a neutral observer, I have to say it's obvious you're the real, true leader."

"Well, just between us, I have to say one thing for sure: Cyclops is a piss-poor leader."

"Yeah?"

"Too distant and shadowy."

"Not moving fast enough?" Adam ventured.

"Oh, we hear about plans to destroy the Great Satan, but nothing happens. No movement. No jihad. Instead, Cyclops is so inept, he lets you, an infidel, sail around the Aegean like you own the place, picking off our boats, our people. Grabbing my nukes. Well, this is my territory. You don't belong here. You're not welcome. And I'm putting an end to your sacrilege."

Just then there was a commotion above them. Faint sounds of bodies hitting the deck. "Enough of this," Roxanna said as she left the cabin. "When I get back, you start talking, really talking, or I start cutting."

CHAPTER 23

MONEMVASIA

Alone in the room, Adam strained against his bindings. He wrenched, twisted, and pulled until his muscles quivered and blood covered his hands and feet, oozing from where the ropes cut his wrists and ankles. He tried to tip the chair over by throwing his weight from side-to-side, but it was too stable. Too big, wide, and solid.

Could he attract attention from other boats by shouting at the top of his lungs? Bad idea. The door, walls, and ceiling around him were at least semi-soundproofed with thick corrugated foam insulation. The neighboring boats were part of the Cyclopean *jamaat* fleet. And worst of all, yelling would probably bring Roxanna back all the sooner, wielding her blade and wire cutters.

Then, the 118-foot *Helios* rocked from side-to-side. Had to be from the wake of a passing ship. For such a large boat, the degree of roll was unusual. But the caique was narrow for its length. *Hmmm.*

Maybe, just maybe. Adam got ready, bided his time, and waited for the next wake. And waited. Yes, a sound. Was it Roxanna coming back with her knife and cutters? He tried to push the thought away. *Come on. Come on. Give me a big wake.*

Finally, one came. The ship heeled far over. Adam threw himself violently to one side, going with it. The chair rocked up on two legs. Teetered. Then banged down again right-side up.

What was that? Footsteps. He froze. Was it Roxanna coming back to flay him alive?

Steeling himself, he waited. The padded door vibrated like it was about to fly open. The slightest sound triggered images of the blade and cutters. He waited, dripping sweat, wrists and ankles screaming with pain, hands and feet dripping blood.

At long last, a big wake came. A truly big wake. Adam threw his weight to one side, going with the roll. The chair tipped up, balanced, teetered for a second time, then finally went on over. Crash. Tied up, there was no way he could soften the blow. But at least he was able to take it on his shoulder, not his head.

On his side, Adam shimmied and squirmed his bound arms off the chair back. Then, rolling onto his back, giving thanks he'd always been flexible, he brought his knees to his chest and passed his bound wrists around over his feet. Once his hands were to his front, he untied the blood-soaked knots with his teeth, hardly noticing the iron taste of his own blood. Then he untied his ankles.

He grabbed a pair of black shorts off a peg up near the low ceiling, and pulled them on. Cracking open the cabin door, he looked fore and aft along a wide passageway. All seemed quiet. Stepping into the walkway, he moved silently toward a stairway. A cabin door behind him opened. He whirled to see a man pop into the hallway. A very big, very fast man. The guy charged straight at him, throwing a haymaker punch, putting his whole body into it. The attack was wild and fierce, but unsophisticated. Knowing just what to do, Adam stepped inside the swing, moved in close and slammed an elbow directly into the guy's face, breaking some facial bones and knocking him out cold.

Adam turned to see a second man pound down the stairway with a glass jug. Charging forward with the hefty bottle upraised, the guy swung it down in a powerful motion, aiming to bash in Adam's head. Another enthusiastic attempt, but artless. Adam guided the swing down to one side, and drove an elbow into the guy's throat, sending him sprawling, choking. A follow-up stomp to the throat left the man quiet and immobile.

Taking the stairs three at a time, Adam climbed into the main salon. A woman with fierce eyes rushed him head on, aiming a powerful kick at his groin. Her face distorted with hatred, determined to incapacitate him, she threw her whole being into the kick. Adam stepped to the side, brought an arm to the back of her neck and used her own momentum to slam her down onto the deck, knocking her out cold.

Moving out onto the stern deck, Adam looked along the quay. Roxanna and a dozen or so men were walking toward *Helios*. Seeing him, she and her men drew weapons and began running, coming fast.

Adam threw off the stern mooring lines, raced to the helm and searched for the engine controls. Where the hell where they? *There*. Low on the rear bulkhead of the main cabin. Shots rang out just as he bent down to reach the engine start button. Bullets whizzed by inches above his back. He pressed the button, staying low. Nothing. He held the button down. *Come on. Come on.* Still nothing. Then he saw a key on a hook below the wheel. More shots. Running feet, getting closer. Snatching the key, he jammed it into what he hoped was the ignition. Turning it, he pressed the button again. One hell of a big engine roared to life.

Ratta-tat-tat. Ratta-tat-tat. Bullets ripped into the binnacle and ship's wheel above him. Footfalls louder and louder. Pressing himself flat onto the deck of the cockpit, Adam reached up one hand to push the throttle full forward. Amazing. *Helios* leapt forward. Hundred-and-eighteen-foot ships didn't do that. But this terrorist boat did. In the nick of time.

As *Helios* pulled away, the fastest terrorist runner leapt from the quay and caught the stern rail. Adam grabbed a winch lever.

Taking aim, he sent the heavy, two-foot metal bar flying at the guy's head, clobbering him in the temple, toppling him into the bay.

Bullets continued to fly. Jihadis scrambled over the two neighboring boats, racing to catch up as *Helios* surged out from between them. One man with the agility of an NFL broken field runner darted along the deck of the boat on *Helios'* port side, caught up, jumped, hoisted himself up over the portside stern, and pulled out a pistol. As the boarder swung the gun up, Adam sent a six-foot wooden boat hook deep into his left eye, tipping him back into the water, screaming.

Two hundred yards out, the caique slowed and spun 180 degrees. Of course; the anchor was forcing the boat to rotate. The good thing was, as the ship turned, Adam's position in the stern became less exposed. With the bow pointed toward the quay and the cabin between him and the terrorist's guns, he rose up enough to reverse the engine and activate the windlass to bring up the anchor. As soon as the hook came off the bottom, the ship raced backward, accelerating away from the quay.

But the terrorists swarmed aboard the two neighboring boats, cast off lines, and came after him, guns blazing. So much for being covert. Where the hell were the Greek police and coast guard? Clearly, the Greek authorities weren't going to be any help. At least in the short run.

Not wanting to slow down to turn around while in gun range, Adam continued flooring it in reverse. He had never experienced anything like the power of the *Helios* engine, especially on a sailboat. Roxanna and the Cyclops crew had transformed the old caique into something akin to a super-fast cigarette boat. *Ha*. They had to be pissed now, as they watched Adam spin the stern to starboard, throw the throttle full forward, and race bow-first from Ormos Milou out onto the windswept Aegean.

Uh-oh. Instead of being left in the dust and disappearing in the distance, the two jihadi boats gave chase with a vengeance. Adam had the engine thundering, pushed to its max with throttle wide open, but the terrorists were keeping up. *Can't lead them back to Dream Voyager.* So, he turned in the opposite direction, heading west. Milos was the southwestern-most island of the Cyclades. Ahead, to the west, was wide open sea. Nothing for eighty miles until you came to the Peloponnesian Peninsula.

He found a pair of range-finder binoculars and studied his pursuers. *Helios* had incredible speed, but so did they. As he scanned the scene behind him, his heart sank even further. A third boat had joined the other two. Then he saw a fourth. All moving with amazing speed. All slowly gaining on him.

Not good. Not good at all. Adam turned on *Helios*' VHF marine radio and sent out an SOS. Over and over. "Mayday. Mayday. I'm under attack. I repeat, I'm under attack." He repeated *Helios*' description, location, direction, and speed. Pled over and over for emergency help. But there was no response. Where was the Greek Coast Guard? Where was anybody? This was modern day Greece. How could this be?

Well, if he couldn't get help, and he couldn't outrun his pursuers, he'd have to figure out some other way to survive.

First, he activated the autopilot on a heading of due west, with the engine cranked wide open to the max. Next, he pulled line from a deck locker and secured the three unconscious terrorists, binding their hands and feet behind their backs and locking them in separate cabins. *Helios*, he found, had an abundance of below-the-waterline cabins well-suited to locking people up.

Then, in between frequent dashes up to the wheel to keep tabs on his pursuers, he searched the ship from main deck to bilges, from stem to stern. He had to take stock of his situation, see what he had to work with.

Helios was an oddball combination of old and new. Its two masts and long, but narrow hull, were crafted of fine hardwood using centuries-old methods. Yet its electronics and engine were state-of-the-art. The Raymarine radar screen—when he switched it on—showed his pursuers slowly closing in with terrible clarity.

The ship's power plant was out of this world. A Vericor TS50 gas turbine 36,000-horsepower Rolls Royce engine fed enormous Kamiwa water jets, essentially turning *Helios* into a giant jet ski. Unfortunately, the terrorist's boats hot on his tail apparently had something even better.

He found three cabins filled to their ceilings with weapons and cash galore. Enough to execute and finance a small war. One cabin was crammed full of what appeared to be ancient Greek art and antiquities.

He discovered and put on long pants and a jacket that fit him in another cabin, but no shoes. He also found his earpiece headset. Pulling it on, he tried calling Tripnee and Sophia, but got no answer.

In a crawl space on the ship's lowest level, he almost overlooked a cleverly concealed compartment built into the ship's massive keel. Using a pry bar, and a hammer and chisel from a workbench in the engine room, he forced it open and *voila*! Amazing: three suitcase nuclear weapons.

Talk about overconfidence. The Cyclopeans had been stupid to keep three nukes on the boat they were using as bait. So now he had them. But for how long? Ever the optimist—after all, what was the alternative? Give up?—he jammed the bombs into a big duffle bag, which he lugged up into the ship's main salon. He resolved not to let the devices fall back into the clutches of the terrorists. No matter what.

Up on deck, he frowned. The *meltemi* was blasting at 30 knots and rising. Big, steep, wind-driven rollers marched down out of the north. The four Cyclopean boats pounded through the rough sea, drawing closer and closer. Try as he might, Adam couldn't outrun them. What was he going to do?

Suddenly, without warning, a rogue wave six or seven times the size of those around it rose up and slammed his starboard side, inundating the entire deck, rolling *Helios* onto its beam ends, flat on its side. Immersed in flying spume, Adam fell down and down through the foam. The ship's wheel, instruments, winches and cockpit flew by—until he slammed into the far portside railing. Underwater, he seized the lifeline and held on for dear life. Would the boat right itself? At last, yes, the long, narrow hull rolled right-side up. Stunned and bruised, but okay, he gave thanks he had not gone overboard. Was he lucky or what?

Helios was a mess. Everything not tied down throughout the ship had gone flying. Chagrined that he had not done so earlier, Adam dug through lockers until he found a life jacket, harness, and tether. Putting these on and clipping himself to the binnacle, he breathed easier.

Helios continued to crash forward toward the western horizon. Riding his bucking, stolen ship, he braced himself and clung to the binnacle as, like a living beast, it jumped and dove, now half submerged, now leaping skyward. He looked out across marching, cresting, relentlessly oncoming rollers stretching to the horizon. With heart pounding and fear dancing up his spine, he was—amazingly yet undeniably—thrilled to be there, elated to be alive.

Hey, did that wave capsize or at least slow his pursuers? He looked back through the spray-filled sea scape. There they were, still right-side up, still racing toward him, getting ever closer.

He forged on, desperately casting about for some way to

survive. The boat stayed upright, bucking through the waves. But the terrorists kept closing the distance, until they breathed down his neck just a quarter mile back.

It was then that Adam glimpsed the hazy outline of land ahead. Coming into view in the distance was the fortified medieval city of Monemvasia. He'd read about the place. Fascinated, he studied it through powerful binoculars. Ah-ha! The seed of an idea came to him. At first it scratched hesitantly at the back of his mind, then popped up fully planned.

At that moment his headset came to life. It was Tripnee and Sophia.

"We saw you tear out of Milos on *Helios*. Are you okay?"

"What about you? Are you okay?"

The women told him how they'd created the diversion that had enabled Adam to get loose and steal away on *Helios*. After explaining his situation, he told them about his idea and they made a plan. Desperate, crazy, and for him probably suicidal. But he grinned. At least he'd go down fighting.

Monemvasia was a towering island mountain fortress connected to the Peloponnesian mainland by a single narrow half-mile-long causeway. The very name said it all—and had given him his idea: *monem* meant single, and *vasia* meant entry. Single entry. The ancient city was built up the side and on top of a massive steep-sided mountain that jabbed up like a great thumb out of the Aegean. Once the westernmost outpost of the Byzantine Empire, the fortress could be approached only one way: via the narrow causeway and through a single gate. He remembered reading that nine hundred years earlier the causeway had had a drawbridge. Now the drawbridge was no more, but the gate remained.

The crucial, amazing thing was, in ancient times a handful of monks had been able to hold off whole attacking armies in

Monemvasia. He just might have a chance to do the same, if he could close that gate in time.

Keeping the engines at full throttle, he adjusted the auto pilot to send *Helios* in an arc around to the south. Then he raced below on bare feet to frantically fill duffle bags with a few select weapons, a whole lot of ammo and a laptop with who-knew-what crucial intel. Returning to the wheel, he made one final adjustment to the auto pilot, then he plopped down on the deck with his back to the cabin bulkhead, bracing for impact, the nukes, weapons, and ammo beside him.

CHAPTER 24

THE STANDOFF

The hundred-eighteen-foot ship slammed into the rocky shore—and kept going. In a cacophony of crashing and splintering, the ship's underbelly stove in, grinding into debris, while the high bow, upper hull, deck, masts, and superstructure clung together and, shrieking in a death scream, thundered up the slope onto the causeway. Finally, its tremendous momentum spent, the hulk came to rest astride the narrow spit of land halfway between the Peloponnese mainland and the island mountain fortress.

One thing for sure: This boat wouldn't be going on any more terrorist missions.

The moment *Helios* came to rest, Adam strapped the bag of nukes on his back, grabbed the duffle bags crammed with weapons, tools, and ammo, and jumped off the broken hulk. Sharp, loose stones covering the roadway cut into his bare feet. Ignoring the pain, he ran as fast as he could toward Monemvasia.

The final hundred yards of the approach road squeezed between surging waves on one side and a towering vertical cliff on the other. Then it came to a stone archway and entry tunnel with a massive open iron gate. The ancient door looked like it hadn't been closed in centuries, its colossal hinges frozen solid. Fortunately, he had tools: the pry bar, and a hammer and chisel off *Helios*. It was also lucky that the terrorists pursuing him would be slowed by having to circle clear around to the quay on the north side of the causeway in Monemvasia Bay, the nearest mooring. But that wouldn't delay them for long.

He set to work with the pry bar, which was long and stout. *Give me a big enough lever and I'll move the earth.* He pried at the gate by wedging in the tip of the bar, feet planted on the wall, hands gripping the bar, and his body horizontal, he strained until the veins popped out of his arms, back and legs, until his muscles quivered with effort. But the gate didn't budge. Then he banged away with sledge hammer and chisel. Huge, powerful blows. Ten. Twenty. Thirty. Nothing. With time running out, his shaky plan seemed doomed. If he couldn't close this rusty old portal, both he and his plan were kaput. Sweat poured off his face and torso, while cold spread through his gut.

Then an idea came to him. He dug into a duffle and pulled out two grenades. He jammed one high and one low between the colossal door and the rock wall behind it, and pulled the pins—making sure to do so simultaneously—and quickly ducked around a corner out of blast range. *Ka-blam*! *Voilà.* The gate swung free. Adam pushed it closed and dropped an ancient crossbar in place to hold it shut.

Gathering up the duffles, he hastened on into the Byzantine city, which seemed eerily deserted. Just like with the gunfights at Kalamaki and Milos, people here were quick to disappear. Was it his imagination or was there an underlying tension in the air? An awareness the world had become a dangerous powder keg. An ever-present fear that any place, at any time, could suddenly be transformed into a war zone—by an explosion, a truck slamming into a crowd, or a ship crashing ashore with terrorists in hot pursuit. And where the hell were the Greek authorities? Hiding like everyone else? Maybe somehow in on it?

Adam ran up a narrow, meandering street of time-polished marble. At last, something that felt good on his tender feet.

Empty cafés, hotels, tavernas, and curio shops occupied ancient cave-like spaces carved into the mountain. He ran on, struggling under his load. Time was running out.

Then: Holy Byzantine mackerel! Just what he needed: a four-wheeled motorcycle with a luggage rack. A game-changer. No ignition key. But he hadn't gone through black ops training for nothing. He threw his gear on the rack and set to work hot-wiring the ignition. In two minutes, the quad bike roared to life, and he was off, rolling past Byzantine churches, climbing meandering streets, working his way up the mountain. As he went, he keyed his radio, trying to reach Tripnee and Sophia, with no luck.

In minutes, he peered down from the mountaintop overlooking the causeway and approach road. Three of the boats had already docked at the quay jutting north from the causeway, their crews even then swarming over the hulk of *Helios* and headed for the iron gate.

It must have been at this very spot in centuries past that stalwart monks had successfully defended Monemvasia against entire armies, shooting crossbows, pouring caldrons of boiling oil, hurling rocks, rolling down boulders. They'd been so successful the stronghold had never been taken in battle. Adam, of course, was just one man. But he had some duffle bags.

He activated his radio again and tried to contact Tripnee and Sophia, but still got no answer. Without them, he—and his plan—were doomed. But he could at least take a whole lot of terrorists down with him. Ignoring the pain of his now bloody feet on the craggy mountaintop, he crept to a place of concealment that had good visibility, where he laid out weapons, clips of ammo, and grenades.

Jihadis ran toward the gate far below, several yelling *Allahu Akbar!* Seeing about a half dozen bunch up in front of the gate, he lobbed a grenade straight down into their midst. *Ka-blam.*

Peering down, he saw torn bodies strewn about, some screaming, others dead as doornails.

Attackers farther back took cover, ducking behind rocks and a concrete block structure at water's edge. Adam picked up an AK-47. With single, careful shots, he picked off first one, then another, then a third.

Jihadis took aim and fired up at him, their bullets missing by inches, one parting his hair. But he persisted. Keeping low, using the cover of the rocks, shooting carefully, he kept the attackers pinned down and stopped their advance.

It was a Mexican standoff for several hours, but the sun was sinking fast. Once darkness fell, how was he going to hold them off? One of the items he had grabbed on *Helios* was an old, rather crummy night-vision monocle, which was better than nothing, but not by much. Very likely, unless the Greek police or military showed up, it was only a matter of time before he was overrun.

Speaking of Greek authorities, where the hell were they? Hey, a line of vehicles was rolling along the causeway, coming out from the distant mainland. Four big, serious-looking SUVs. Adam's spirits lifted. Help had arrived. Although the cars had no official markings, they had an air of, what? Authority, organization, and purpose. The official-looking caravan stopped at the quay, just out of AK-47 range, and disgorged, uh-oh, twenty or so more terrorists.

If that wasn't bad enough, right then, in the darkening twilight, a fourth boat—and soon a fifth, and then a sixth—docked at the quay, all loaded with armed fighters, clearly not friendlies. An opaque darkness descended. Squinting through the low-budget night-vision monocle, he made out vague shapes moving about, getting ready.

Testing the range of the AK-47, Adam let loose a fierce barrage at the quay, the boats, the vehicles. As he burned through clip after clip, most of his bullets fell short, but a few of his rounds found targets, which seemed to slow the activity on the quay and around the cars. Or had they just become more stealthy?

Movement. Down on the road approaching the gate. Adam moved to a place where he could peer straight down on the road. No sooner had he changed locations, than a small rocket, probably a rocket-propelled grenade, streaked up and exploded in the spot where he'd been moments before.

Adam emptied three clips of ammo into the spot from which the rocket had been launched. Then, quickly, he moved a second time. And thank God. Three RPG rockets, coming from three different launch points, shot up and exploded where he'd been seconds before.

Then three rockets hit the gate. The fiery explosions lit up the scene far below and rattled the base of the mountain. But the mammoth old gate held.

Adam let loose several full clips down at the rocket launch points and then jumped to a new location on the clifftop. The reply was swift. More rockets blasted his previous location, engulfing it in flames.

More rockets hit the gate. One, two, three, four. But, by the light of the flames, he saw it was still there. *They sure don't make gates like that anymore.* Adam's gaze hardened and his heart sank. As more and more rockets streaked in to pound the ancient portal, inevitably, eventually, something had to give. It was the hinges. First the top one gave way, then the bottom, then the middle.

Fighters swarmed forward, charging the gate. Adam threw his last remaining grenades and risked a quick burst from his AK-47 to slow them down, but soon two missiles shot toward him. He jumped right and they went wide to his left. But he knew he was done for. The RPG launchers had figured out their timing. Now that the entry was breached, they sat there ready, poised but holding their fire, just waiting for him to reveal his location. Without doubt, his next blast from the AK-47 would be his last. Well, so be it. Go down fighting. In preparation for the end, for his final battle, he opened the cases of the three nukes next to him, so any blast that killed him would render them inoperable.

He looked down. Flames lit the scene below enough for him to let loose one last hail of lead down on the terrorists rushing the open gate. He took aim at the lead guy, the man closest to the gate. Amazingly—before he could fire, the guy's head exploded. Then the second guy's head disappeared as well. Then the third. This turned the tide. The attackers swung around and ran back toward their boats and vehicles.

His heart leaping with relief and joy, Adam looked toward the mainland, high up the mountain. Yes. Tiny flashes accompanied by faint, distant popping sounds. It had to be Tripnee.

Amazing sharp cookie that she was, after stopping the charge, she immediately took out the rocket launchers. This done, she went to work on the cars and boats, which began to explode and burst into flames. A pack of terrorists tried charging along the causeway back toward the mainland, intent on taking out this new shooter on the mountain. But the men leading this group started dropping like flies, turning the others back. Jihadis scrambled toward the remaining boats, cast off lines, and began motoring away. More boats burst into flame. Four sank. But two got away into the blustering night.

CHAPTER 25

LIMENAS GERAKA

Ecstatic to still be breathing, Adam drove the four-wheel motor bike down off Monemvasia. The howling *meltemi* felt invigorating. The sting of gnarly metal foot mounts gouging his bloody, throbbing feet was not only not a problem, it was totally okay. What did pain matter? He was alive.

As he maneuvered down steep switchbacks, Adam re-established radio contact with Tripnee and Sophia, and they made a plan. Tripnee would stay in place high up the mountain slope on the mainland ready to ward off any returning terrorists. Sophia would bring *Dream Voyager* in off the windswept Aegean to Monemvasia quay. Adam would meet the boat at the quay, help with the docking, and then dive down to the sunken terrorist's wrecks to search for nukes and information.

The ancient iron gate lay twisted, battered, and far enough ajar for him to accelerate straight through and out along the causeway. But the road was blocked by the *Helios'* shattered hulk. Testing the quad bike's limits, he drove off the roadway down the boulder-strewn slope to the water's edge. Here, timing his move between waves, he gunned the bike through foot-deep water, hoping to squeeze past the crumpled bow. The wheels spun at the halfway, deepest point, spewing seawater, going nowhere. *Uh-oh.* An extra big wave reared up, sweeping toward him. Finally, a moment before the wave hit, the tires caught, propelling the bike up the steep slope out of its reach.

Back up on the roadway, he stopped the bike and pulled himself up onto *Helios*. He hobbled through the wreck, leaving bloody footprints. As he suspected, the three prisoners he'd tied up were gone. Also gone were any additional laptops or documents. Too bad, they might have had intel crucial to rounding up the remaining nukes and maybe the whole *jamaat*.

Adam drove out onto the quay just as Sophia maneuvered *Dream Voyager* alongside. Incoming rollers kicked up by the howling *meltemi* whipped the boat up, down, and sideways, smashing it against the unyielding stone dock. Fortunately, Sophia had put out a full set of fenders, which cushioned the impact. Also, she'd coiled mooring lines on the starboard bow and stern. Forgetting his lacerated feet, Adam, watching for his chance, grabbed and secured the stern line to a bollard, then did the same with the bow line.

Adam climbed aboard *Dream Voyager,* lugging the laptop and three nukes. Sophia took one look at his blood-caked ankles and wrists and bloody feet, and made him sit down so she could clean and bandage his wounds. Again, something about her gaze, when their eyes met ever so briefly, made him look away.

"Are those two prisoners from *Bora* still aboard?"

"They got free and attacked me," Sophia said in her matter of fact way. "I had to shoot 'em. Then I tied weights to the bodies, and rolled 'em overboard."

Time to search the sunken boats. Adam pulled on his wet suit, mask, rebreather, headlamp, and, wincing, swim fins. First, he dove on the three boats sitting on the bottom adjacent to the quay. All three had exploded and been gutted by fire, leaving no useful clues. And despite an inch-by-inch search, he found no nukes.

The fourth boat, submerged a hundred yards from the quay, was a similar story—except for a still-intact waterproof case. Grabbing it, he swam for the surface and back to *Dream Voyager*.

Time to get out of there. With the wind screaming, the sea surging, and the boat leaping erratically, Adam and Sophia powered north eleven miles. Driving upwind the whole way, they pounded straight into foam-spewing rollers up the Peloponnese coast to Limenas Geraka, a quaint little town nestled in a deep, hidden, wonderfully still fjord. Here they Med-moored alongside a half dozen other boats, and met Tripnee, who had traveled overland from her sniper's aerie.

As night turned to day, Adam and Tripnee stretched out on the cockpit cushions while Sophia dug into the ship's freezer and pantry to prepare and serve a downright fabulous meal of ribeye steak, sweet potatoes, and canned vegetables. Surprising and delightful.

The trio savored the quiet of the fjord. Exhausted but too wound up to sleep, they sipped wine and talked about their perilous previous twenty-four hours.

Tripnee said, "The boats that got away were the *Al-Gazi*"

"The *Al-Gazi*," Adam said. "was the big, austere karavoskara we saw at Finikas. I had a bad feeling about that boat."

"Yeah, me, too."

And the other boat?"

"Was *The Crescent Moon*. Get it? Symbol of Islam." Tripnee turned to Sophia. "Did you fly drones onto the boats that got away?"

"No, the winds were too strong and erratic."

Adam said, "The terrorists just lost a lot of people and boats. They have to be reeling and need to regroup. But my guess is they'll be more determined than ever to use their two remaining nukes."

Sophia nodded. "Can you imagine what just the two remaining bombs could do? One in New York and one in London?"

With renewed desperation to find the remaining nukes, they poured through the paper documents from the watertight case.

"I can't read any of this stuff," Adam said.

"Me, neither," Tripnee said.

"It's what they do," Sophia said. "Everything is written in unreadable code."

The three of them turned to contemplate the *Helios* laptop. What in hell was the password?

Struck by a thought, Adam said, "It can't be," but typed in "Allahu Akbar." Amazingly, that was it. He scrolled through a seemingly endless list of the computer's files, a treasure trove of information sure to bring down the Cyclops *jamaat* and save the lives of millions, maybe billions. Talk about euphoria, their spirits soared.

Sophia became especially animated. "Wow. I can't believe you came up with the password."

But it was so *much* information, it would take days, maybe weeks to go through it. Adam's exhilaration gave way to a realization this was going take time, patience, and sustained alertness. Suddenly, his deep exhaustion caught up with him. Barely able to keep his eyes open, he stumbled below, stretched out, and instantly plunged into deep sleep.

He popped wide awake in the middle of the afternoon. His feet, wrists, and ankles were still on fire, but he felt refreshed and eager to begin pouring through the digital files. Careful not to disturb Tripnee, who was snoring softly, he limped into the salon where he found and opened the laptop.

Strange. Unbelievable. The computer's files had disappeared. Completely. Maybe deleted by a security program? Clever, devious, and tech-savvy—how could these people be so determined to murder millions?

More resolved than ever, but increasingly frantic, Adam reached for the waterproof case. The coded material—and the laptop and phone from *Deniz*—would have to be hacked and deciphered by Admiral Jeppesen's people back in Washington DC. But that would take time that they did not have. So, he continued studying the documents, determined to find some telltale clue, something, anything. He examined every scrap of paper, front and back, until the salon table was covered with the coded documents, and the case sat empty.

Hmmm. Running his hands over the case's inner lining, he felt a slight bulge. Getting a screwdriver, he pried up the lining bottom. *Voilà*. Adam found himself holding Greek Coast Guard registry papers for the sunken 74-foot terrorist motor-sailer ketch *Crescent Moon* and also a small card with a snippet of cryptic directions to a location on the island of Spetsai.

CHAPTER 26

SPETSAI

Tripnee, yawning and stretching, sat down beside Adam at the salon table. After telling her the computer had mysteriously been wiped clean, Adam showed her the card and the boat's registry papers.

"Interesting," he said, "both point to the island of Spetsai, north of here."

"The two boats that got away," Tripnee said, "raced off in that direction."

"That settles it. Next stop, Spetsai."

With Sophia still asleep in her cabin, Adam and Tripnee brought in the mooring lines, weighed anchor, and skimmed quietly out of the idyllic fjord. The wind remained strong on the open sea. Adam set a course toward Spetsai, sails close-hauled, across the mouth of the Gulf of Argolis, some thirty-two miles distant.

Sophia burst up the companionway and marched into the cockpit. "It's too rough. The forecast shows fifty-knot *meltemis* strafing the Cyclades for the next three days."

Tripnee turned to Adam. "Are you nuts? You know I hate sailing in that."

Adam looked at Sophia with mild surprise. Then he said, "The Cyclades are eighty miles east of us. Here, we're way over on the fringe of that weather system. And the farther north we sail, the closer we get to the Saronic Gulf around Athens, the more protected we'll be from the wind."

Only partially mollified, the women took up positions in the cockpit, sullenly eyeing the weather. Well, at least the two of them were bonding over something. But why did it have to be against him?

As they moved north, sure enough, the wind did gradually decrease. After a while, looking considerably more cheerful, Tripnee said, "It was in Spetsai and nearby Idra, that the Greek War of Independence against the Ottoman Empire first began in 1821. A big inspiration for the war was an extraordinary woman named Bouboulina, who commanded the Spetsiot fleet."

Sophia frowned, hunched her shoulders and drew her knees up to her chest. "A terrible war."

Undaunted, Tripnee continued, "Local legend, which I read about in your Greek Waters book, Adam, has it that Bouboulina was one gutsy woman. Without her, the Greeks never would have won. It was Bouboulina who destroyed the Turkish fleet at Navplion with fire ships."

"Gotta like it," Adam said.

"Not," Sophia harrumphed.

Standing and strutting a bit, Tripnee said, "It goes to show that if you can skipper one ship, others may join you. And if you lead a fleet, you can forge a new future."

"Okay," Sophia said, "it does that."

Spetsai came into view late in the afternoon. The hilly six- by four-mile island was dotted by a sparse pine forest.

Perhaps making an effort to be more sociable, Sophia said, "They made a big effort to plant all those trees, but neglected to water them. So, they're barely alive."

"Sounds like you know the island," Adam said. "What else can you tell us?"

Sophia smiled broadly. "It's an interesting place. The main harbor and town around on the far side are popular with tourists. One reason being no motor vehicles, except motorbikes, are allowed."

"It wouldn't be good to sail into the center of things," mused Adam. "Better to anchor somewhere out of the way."

A little after sunset, they dropped anchor in a small cove on the west side of Zoyioryia Bay, at the far northwest end of the island. Below deck, each filled a backpack with the particular tools matching their skill set. Then, in the twilight, they dug three mountain bikes out of a stern lazerette, loaded them into the dinghy, and motored to a sheltered beach. Dragging the skiff well up from the water, they pulled on their packs and carried the bikes up through the woods lining the shoreline to a road that, according to their map, circled the island.

An old man hummed by on a Vespa motor scooter.

Not knowing who to trust, and not wanting to alert their quarry, they chose not to ask directions. Instead, they set off on the bikes determined to figure out the card's enigmatic directions with no help from locals.

Sophia lagged behind. Over their earpiece radios, she said, "A little card with the words, 'Red gate west Spetsai' isn't enough to go on."

"I dunno," Adam said. "Why hide the card if it's not important?"

"It's definitely worth checking out," Tripnee said.

Sophia's silence spoke volumes, and she made no effort to catch up.

"Adam and I can handle this just fine," Tripnee said. "We'll meet you back at the boat."

Sophia smoldered for a while, muttering, but then caught up.

"Hey," Adam said, "we're a team, remember?"

As the road followed the steep mountainous southern

shoreline, it undulated up and down and snaked around bend after bend. Pedaling through the deepening twilight, they shined their headlamps on gate after gate, but none were red. Until, after several miles, there it was, a red gate. Seemed a little too simple, really. But, who knew?

The driveway beyond the gate led down onto a promontory that jutted out into the Argolic Gulf. Getting out his night-vision goggles, Adam saw a stately white villa on the headland and, far below to the right and left, idyllic beaches lapped by gentle waves.

What's that? The rumble of motorcycles. The trio scrambled to get their bicycles off the road behind a clump of bushes. They'd just ducked out of sight when a group of motorcyclists pulled up at the gate. Adam, peering through the foliage, recognized the beard, the straight black hair, the scowl of one of the men—it was Basham Bilel, captain of the *Al-Gazi*.

The bikers opened the gate, drove through, closed and locked it behind them, and continued down out onto the headland. But they did not go clear to the house. Instead, midway, they turned off on some sort of spur road, and dropped out of sight as they traversed across the steep mountainside.

"Fuck, shit, hell," Tripnee blurted out. "Déja vu. I read about this place. This is Villa Yasemia. It's the setting for *The Magus*. And it's where John Fowles wrote the book."

"Yeah? Amazing."

Adam and Tripnee, with guns drawn and night-vision goggles in place, crossed the road, climbed over the gate, and followed the bikers. Sophia stayed behind, both as lookout and to deploy her drones.

The narrow spur trail was nearly invisible and would have been almost impossible to find if they had not seen the motorcycles turn onto it moments before. The hard rock surface showed no tire tracks that Adam could see. But Tripnee, drawing on her childhood experience tracking game with her Choinumni shaman father, intuitively, instinctively sussed out the path as it snaked across the steep slope. Abruptly, the trail ended in an expanse of smooth rock.

Studying the blank stone, Adam detected the edges, the outline, of a huge hidden door. Silently pointing it out to Tripnee, he motioned for them to withdraw. Fifty yards away, they hunkered down among boulders.

"It's coming back to me," Tripnee whispered. "In the novel, Fowles wrote about secret underground bunkers built here by the Nazis during World War II. I assumed they were fictitious. But they're actually real."

"Could be the gang's main headquarters," Adam whispered. "Might be enough intel here to round up the entire organization. And maybe the last two bombs."

Tripnee was exultant and amped up, "At last. The nerve center. After all this effort. After you almost getting killed over and over. What a fucking ordeal. But this makes it all worth it."

Adam smiled, nodding.

Tripnee kept on, "Finally. Our persistence has paid off. We've just found the whole shebang—including, I hope to God, the last two bombs."

"Trouble is," Adam said, "how're we gonna quietly get through that rock door? We've got to find a back entrance, another way in."

Adam looked around for any drones, but saw none. Assuming their drone falconer teammate was listening in over her earpiece—and probably watching through a drone camera, he asked, "Sophia, are you tracking this? I think we've found a whole cave complex. Can you use a heat-sensing drone to find a ventilation tunnel or a back door or something?"

Oddly, there was no response.

Adam repeated his questions, but again there was only silence. Something was wrong. He and Tripnee started up the trail to check on Sophia.

KA-BLAAAAM

Behind them, a huge explosion blew the massive stone door clean away. Taking off their night goggles, they watched towering flames pour up from the opening, leaping forty and fifty feet into the night sky. As they backed away, more explosions deep in the cave complex shook the earth. The flames raged, growing in intensity. Then several smaller columns of flame rose up in the near distance around them. Probably the secondary entrances Adam had asked Sophia to find.

His heart sank. Another treasure trove of information lost. But was Sophia okay?

"Sophia, are you okay?"

They turned again to race back up the trail.

Suddenly, Sophia's sweetly accented voice sounded in their earpieces, "I'm okay. Don't worry about me. See if we can salvage anything from that cave hideout."

Breathing a sigh of relief, Adam turned again to study the flames, but he and Tripnee were driven back by the intense heat, which seemed to only grow stronger and stronger.

CHAPTER 27

BALTIZA CREEK

Adam paced back and forth in *Dream Voyager*'s main salon, pondering the cave inferno and the erased laptop. "All that intel lost."

Sophia, working at the stern end of the massive salon table, silently sent drones up the companionway. Out in the morning air, the tiny quadracopters buzzed away to search Spetsai for *Al-Gazi* and *The Crescent Moon*—and for any and all terrorists in the Interpol database.

After a while, she said, "The members have to be reeling, staggering. They just lost their nerve center and a lot of key people. And that's on top of all the bombs, boats, and people we took down before that."

Cleaning her M82 at the opposite end of the table, Tripnee said through clenched teeth, "They've still got two bombs. We've absolutely got to find 'em."

Sophia spat out, "That's bleeding obvious." Then, softening, she said, "I've been investigating this terrorist group for years. These people—especially Roxanna—are devious."

"Talk about obvious," Tripnee said, rolling her eyes. "Tell us something we don't know."

"They're also deep, clever, strategic. Roxanna, for instance, is one hell of a chess player. She doesn't just think one or two moves ahead, she thinks five or six moves ahead."

"So, what's she thinking now?" Adam asked.

"A seat-of-the pants person—a less far-sighted leader—would rush to launch their big attack. They'd sail their two remaining bombs straight for the United States."

"And you think she'll do something different?" Adam asked.

"From her perspective, something unknown has devastated her operation," Sophia said. "She still doesn't completely know who or what she's up against."

"And that'll make her cautious?"

"Based on what I know of her, she'll do something you'd never expect. Maybe sail in the opposite direction—or go nowhere—maybe hide in plain sight."

"So much for all your investigating," Tripnee sneered. "That tells us nothing useful."

Sophia bared her perfect teeth. "The thing about Roxanna that we can count on is her ambition. Her determination to advance, build a name for herself, gain followers."

"She's one tough woman all right," Adam said.

"The way you become a great terrorist leader," Sophia continued, "is to strike a mighty blow against the Great Satan. Say, by simultaneously exploding nuclear bombs in New York and San Francisco."

"Duh, talk about the bleeding obvious," Tripnee muttered.

Ignoring this, Sophia continued, "Another thing we can count on: Roxanna will do everything she can to find out who's tracking her and what she's up against."

"Another bleedingly obvious 'insight,'" Tripnee said. "So where does that leave us?"

"One thing," Adam said, "we saw *Al-Gazi*'s captain go into the cave. That means *Al-Gazi* itself is probably around here somewhere." Then, looking at Sophia, he continued, "Drones are good, but there's nothing like being there in person. Especially if they disguise their boats."

The trio rowed their bikes and backpacks ashore a second

time. For some strange reason the hairs on the back of Adam's neck stood up. Why? Looking around carefully, he saw no threats. Not wanting to spook his already on-edge team, he said nothing. But he couldn't shake an uneasy feeling, and remained on high alert.

This time they cycled along the northern coast of Spetsai, checking each cove and anchorage for any sign of the terrorists' boats. It was midmorning when they reached the town of Spetsai at the northeastern end of the island. Here, moving among multitudes of tourists, they looked over Dapia Harbor, which was crowded with ferries, water taxis, and party boats. Adam half expected the place to be buzzing with talk of the explosions of the night before on the other side of the small island. Perhaps because the detonations had occurred underground, or maybe because such events were the new normal, life here seemed to be humming along as usual.

Farther on, they passed through neighborhoods of grand old houses, and then arrived at the heart of the Spetsai boating scene: Baltiza Creek, which consisted of a large outer and a smaller inner harbor.

The whole place was a madhouse. Throughout the outer harbor a vast flotilla of exquisite yachts and humbler craft had been jockeyed into every nook and cranny, filling every possible mooring spot. In the inner harbor, a similar dizzying menagerie of boats was crammed even more tightly together. Lining the shore, boat yards overflowed with yachts up on the hard. So many were being repaired and repainted, you couldn't make out individual craft. It was the perfect place to hide in plain sight— while getting the disguise of a new paint job in the process.

Throngs of people climbed among the boats, packed waterfront tavernas, and filled the streets walking, sitting astride motor scooters, pedaling bikes, and lounging in horse-drawn carriages. This press of human souls overwhelmed Adam's intuitive radar. All the while, deep down, was the feeling he and his team were centered in someone's crosshairs.

To blend in while studying the tumultuous scene, they grabbed a waterfront table and ordered breakfast.

"Something tells me," Sophia said, "it's dangerous for us to be here."

"You should go back to the boat," Tripnee said. "Adam and I can handle this."

"I wouldn't dream of it."

"Hey, cut that out," Adam said. "How many times do I have to say it? We're a team. Right now, the three of us—all three of us—have got to focus on working together. Let's act like this is the most important job in the world."

"Amen," Sophia said. "Because it is."

Continuing, Adam pointed out that it was going to take a combination of drones and leg work to search the harbor. They made a plan. Adam and Tripnee fanned out to walk through the boat yards, studying each hull. Meanwhile, Sophia moved to an out-of-the-way waterfront bench, where, with the aid of her wrist device and glasses, she sent drones to search Baltiza Creek for the enemy.

Adam was on the far side of the harbor when he heard a distant, suppressed "bang."

"I'm hit," Sophia cried over their comms. "I'm hit bad."

Being closer, Tripnee was the first to get back to Sophia. Over his earpiece radio, Adam heard, "You poor dear. You're shot through the shoulder. But you're going to be okay."

By the time Adam arrived, Tripnee, drawing on her medic training, had expertly staunched the flow of blood, applied temporary bandages to the entry and exit wounds, and administered a pain-numbing injection.

Studying Sophia, Adam asked, "How are you?"

Sophia winced, "Damn. I hate it when this happens."

"All considered, this girl is incredibly lucky," Tripnee said. "Had to be an extremely fast, small bullet. It went right through her Kevlar vest, then passed cleanly through, missing the heart, the bones, the major veins, and arteries."

Adam asked, "Did you see the shooter? A muzzle flash?"

"No," Sophia said. "The shot came out of nowhere." Then, sitting up on the bench and looking out over the harbor, she blurted, "Hey. There goes *Al-Gazi*."

Turning around, Adam and Tripnee saw it, too.

A second later, Adam said, "And there's *The Crescent Moon*."

The two boats now had deep blue hulls and white trim, but they were the terrorists' boats, all right. Just then motoring together out of the Baltiza Creek outer harbor—getting clean away—headed out onto the wide Aegean.

"Oh, no, they don't," Sophia muttered through gritted teeth. Still wearing her wrist device and glasses—wincing with pain all the while—she moved her hands through the air, maneuvering her drones. After a few minutes, she leaned back and let out a deep convulsive shudder, saying, "Done. Snuck drones aboard both those cocksuckers."

Tripnee, maybe for the first time, looked on admiringly, "This girl's got grit."

CHAPTER 28

CLOSE-HAULED

Sophia stubbornly refused to be taken to the local hospital. Under normal circumstances, Adam and Tripnee would have nonetheless delivered her to professional medical care. But Tripnee's medic skills were strong and Sophia was not only undaunted and apparently able to function—she was also, well, indispensable. And their mission right then was the most important job in the world. Right?

Adam raced back to *Dream Voyager*, motored around to Baltiza Creek and picked up Sophia and Tripnee. The terrorist's boats were by then out of drone transmission range. But at least they had tracking drones aboard the boats, and if they could guess their direction and they sailed far enough, very likely they could pick them up on Sophia's tracking screen.

Would Roxanna continue her stratagem of doing the unexpected? She had to be seething with anger, and dying to lash out. But most likely she'd reject heading straight for the United States as too obvious.

Instead, wily as she was, she'd probably go in the opposite direction. Not only would she do this to fool her enemies, it would allow her and her people to bide their time, regroup, and learn more about who or what was arrayed against them. Later, when all was ready and her target least expected it, she'd strike. Two nuclear bombs, after all, would suffice to cause enough death and mayhem to be remembered forever.

The shortest route to America was to go south around the Peloponnese Peninsula toward the mouth of the Mediterranean. The opposite direction, the most counterintuitive, was to go east. So, *Dream Voyager* headed east.

While Sophia slept in a pain-killer induced haze below deck, Adam and Tripnee stood watch, with Adam at the wheel and Tripnee studying the drone-tracking screen. Unfortunately, no drones showed up on the display.

Because they were nearing the sheltered Saronic Gulf, the *meltemi* was 18 knots—unlike the 50-knot gale at that moment blasting the Cyclades farther east. To take advantage of these more manageable winds, yachts had migrated in this direction from all over the Greek islands, making this one hell of a popular sailing area, with many very fast boats speeding around in the distance. *Dream Voyager*, for its part, was strutting its stuff and out-performing any boat in sight, doing what few sailboats could do, flying close-hauled and pointing fifteen-degrees to the wind.

"I've gotta say, I'm impressed," Tripnee began. "I think I might owe her an apology."

Adam nodded.

"The girl was shot, drugged up," continued Tripnee.

"And had to be wracked with pain," inserted Adam.

"But nonetheless had the presence of mind to not only see the terrorist boats—"

"Which we totally missed," Adam said.

"But also fly drones aboard."

"If it weren't for her quick wits, we wouldn't have a prayer of finding the last two nukes. In which case, very likely, goodbye San Francisco and New York."

"Even so, it's going to be dicey. This screen's showing no sign of anything."

"Well, let's pray we pick up a signal somewhere ahead. We're approaching Idra. Maybe we'll get lucky."

Sophia appeared from below just then. She moved slowly, clearly in pain, but also clearly determined to carry on. Judging from her sly smile, she'd been listening in for a while.

"The three of us together are for-mee-*dahb*-luh. Roxanna might be one hell of a chess player, but the three of us, we're like an omnipotent ghost. We're going to crush little Roxanna."

"We're picking up two signals," Tripnee yelled. "Both in Idra Harbor."

CHAPTER 29

IDRA

Rod Heikell's *Greek Waters Pilot* showed Idra, also called Hydra, to be a long, high, skinny, arid ridge roughly 10-miles-long east to west, and one- to two-miles-wide north to south. As *Dream Voyager* approached from the west, Adam used powerful binoculars to study Limin Idra, the island's main harbor, located dead center on its north coast. Judging from the dense thicket of masts showing above the harbor mole, or seawall, the place was jam-packed. Another perfect place to hide in plain sight.

"I've been running through the drones' sound-activated recordings from the last few hours," Sophia said. "Listen to this." She played the drone audio feed over *Dream Voyager*'s sound system.

"So far, they've outsmarted us at every turn. We were ready to go, ready to strike. Then they sank *Saadet* on Rinia, torched your boat *Deniz* at Ermoupolis, and sank *Dido*, *Humbaba*, and *Profit* at Paros."

"That's Sahiba Mukadder," Sophia said, "captain of *The Crescent Moon*."

Roxanna said, "They made *Bora* and *Canan* disappear off Folegandros."

Sahiba Mukadder went on, "And they ran *Helios* onto the causeway at Monemvasia, and sank *Show Ya* and *Okay Beer* right there, too."

"Curse them a thousand times," said an unidentified voice, "for blowing up our underground command base on Spetsai. We've been decimated."

"Believe me, I know, I know," Roxanna said. Then whispering, she continued, "But trust me, Allah has not forsaken us. We will destroy the Great Satan. These setbacks only harden our resolve."

"Our faith is strong, sister," Sahiba said, "but what are we going to do? We only have two—only two—bombs left."

"Sssshh," Roxanna whispered. "I think the problem is we either have a mole or we've been bugged. So, keep this between us. We have a trick or two up our sleeve. Tell no one. We have a submarine."

"Praise Allah," whispered the unidentified voice, "a submarine."

"Allahu Akbar," Sahiba whispered. "Where is this submarine?"

"It will meet us here tonight."

Adam, Tripnee, and Sophia looked at one another and nodded. They had their night's work cut out for them.

It wouldn't be a good idea to take *Dream Voyager* into Idra harbor, so they sailed on a mile north and dropped anchor in picturesque, north-facing Mandraki Bay.

Sophia clutched at her shoulder, sweating and shivering.

Adam asked, "How are you doing? Are you up for this?"

"Believe me," she said, steeling herself, "this is right where I want to be."

Glancing at both Tripnee and Sophia, he said, "Something tells me these last two nukes are going to be difficult to get, maybe more difficult than the first eleven. Let's prepare accordingly."

Tripnee, looking serious and grim, agreed, "Amen to that."

Sophia just nodded, still clutching her shoulder.

"Whatever happens," Adam said, "Don't underestimate Roxanna. Expect the unexpected."

"On that note, disguises would be a good precaution," Tripnee said.

Going for a carefree-clueless-sailing-couple look, they drew on his black ops and her undercover FBI training to transform themselves. The result for both: bushy, unkempt, blond hair; loose, sloppy clothing; and garish sunglasses.

Next, they packed weapons and other gear with utmost care, trying to anticipate every possible eventuality. When loaded and ready, the skiff sat low in the water, heavy with extra gear. Adam got into the bow. Tripnee, in the stern, started the engine, motored out of Mandraki Bay and turned left, west. The 25-horsepower outboard, a 15-knot wind, and a pattern of two-foot white-capped rollers pushed them along the steep, rocky coastline toward Limin Idra.

The island's main harbor turned out to be a compact 200-yard by 100-yard rectangular boat basin lined on three sides by shoulder-to-shoulder bars, stores, and *tavernas*. On the fourth, north, side, a seawall, or mole, protected the harbor, leaving a 40-yard-wide opening on the northeast corner.

A huge mass of luxury yachts filled over half the harbor. Jammed tightly together, bunched along the protected side of the mole, this vast clump of fancy vessels was seven and eight boats deep and fifty or so boats across. Threading her way around the sprawling flotilla, Tripnee guided the skiff to a small, inconspicuous dinghy dock in the harbor's far northwest corner, where Adam hopped out and secured their bow line.

All over the quays and mole, and throughout the mass of boats, the scene buzzed and boomed, rocked and rolled with loud music and people yelling, eating, laughing, drinking, dancing, and partying.

Taking with them only concealed, silenced hand guns, and

leaving the rest of their gear in the skiff battened down under a tarp, Adam and Tripnee merged into the boisterous crowd and walked out along the mole. In their guise as the carefree couple, they took pictures, laughed and chatted people up—all while scanning the vast crush of boats for *Al-Gazi* and *The Crescent Moon*. Where the hell were they?

For a while, as they examined the boats in the surrounding area, Adam struck up a conversation with an American couple who were on the sixth year of an around-the-world cruise aboard their 65-foot ketch, *Patriot*. These garrulous souls—who'd been there for a week—were a fountain of information about life in the harbor.

No one in the crush of over three hundred boats was getting much sleep because of the all-night parties. The attitude, though, was relaxed; when someone pulled up a neighbor's anchor because it was hooked to theirs, they just dropped it again and the neighbor merely tightened up a bit on their anchor chain, no problem.

The ethic in Idra was that the harbor wasn't full until it was literally full, wall-to-wall with boats. Walking across other boats in Greece is assumed to be okay; there was no need to ask permission. The confusion of interlinked boats, fenders, mooring lines, anchor chains, and interconnecting planks just seemed to somehow work—with everyone relaxing, living and letting live.

Suddenly, Adam saw *Al-Gazi*, now with new dark blue paint, and a new name emblazoned across its stern, *Tad*. And right next to it was *The Crescent Moon*, now renamed *Lila*. With a tilt of his head, he pointed them out to Tripnee.

"Ah-ha," she whispered. "*Tad* means 'poet,' and *Lila* in Arabic means 'woman of the night.'"

Adam dropped a small waterproof tracking beacon the size of a poker chip into the water.

"Excellent," Sophia whispered into their earpieces. "Good job finding them. I will fly more drones into and around them and keep you posted."

For some reason, at that moment, Adam's attention was drawn to a three-masted, 150-foot dream yacht outside the harbor, on the seaward side of the mole. Smaller boats 80-foot and under moored inside the mole, while mega yachts Med-moored outside it and were exposed to the northern *meltemi*. The wind had increased to maybe 20 knots, but this big boat was still coming in to Med-moor. Why now?

Intrigued, Adam watched the mega yacht maneuver and jockey for position in the white-capped waves and blustery wind 300 yards out from the mole. Suddenly, the mammoth boat pointed its stern to shore, dropped its massive anchor, and, with anchor chain rattling out in a fast and furious roar, it came racing backward toward a narrow slot between two other similar-sized yachts—on which uniformed crews stood poised at the ready with giant, three-foot-diameter, hand-held fenders. The mega yacht came flying straight back into the narrow slot. By using side thrusters, it slid right down the middle, leaving exactly the same space, about four feet, between it and the boats on either side. It stopped in perfect position to toss out stern lines and drop its stern gangplank centered on the three-foot-wide concrete walkway clearly there for this purpose.

Noticing the same boat, Tripnee pointed to the name, "*Galel*, means 'Wave of Allah.'"

"Are you seeing this?" Adam asked Sophia over their comms. "Something about *Galel* is ringing my alarm bells. See if you can get some drones aboard and keep an eye on her crew."

As the sun set, Adam and Tripnee retreated to an outdoor café at the land end of the mole where they could survey the scene without being noticed. To stay in character with their disguises—and also because they were starving—they ordered gyro sandwiches and beer.

Tripnee said, "Roxanna's clever, all right. She had good reason to think we'd never look for her in the middle of this flotilla. And even now that we've found her, we can't very well blow them to smithereens or even initiate a firefight with so many innocent people jammed together close by."

"True, to a degree," Sophia said, speaking over their earpieces. "However, I've got enough drones inside and around all three boats—*Tad, Lila,* and *Galel*—to identify terrorists, direct your fire, and minimize collateral damage."

"To get these last two nukes," Adam said, "we'll have to take some risks. But a big question is: What's Roxanna cooked up?"

"Did you see that?" Tripnee asked. "That little Yoda-like guy with big eyes and ears we saw back on *Deniz* just walked from *Galel* over toward *Tad* and *Lila*. What's his name?"

"Abdul Kareem Aziz," Adam said. "He's Yoda-like, all right. I wonder if he's the captain of *Galel*. Very interesting, indeed."

As twilight descended into a pitch-black moonless night, Adam mulled things over, trying to see every angle. Then he outlined a plan.

Tripnee and Adam returned to the nearby corner of the marina where their skiff, hidden in dark shadow, bobbed in the harbor's tiny, ever-present wave chop. Adam ducked under the tarp to pull on his wetsuit, fins, rebreather, underwater night-vision goggles, and two very full fanny packs.

Meanwhile, Tripnee slid her arms through the shoulder straps of her Barrett M82 carrying case, which, with the rifle stock folded, looked like a big, long backpack. Peering out from under the tarp, Adam found himself, as he often did, admiring his sweetheart's toughness. Carrying an M82 with ammo was normally the job of two men in the U.S. Army, but this amazing woman did it alone, without complaint, with a spring in her step.

Tripnee walked up several steep back streets, entered the biggest, highest building overlooking Idra harbor, and began climbing stairs to the rooftop.

Adam slid into the water, adjusted his rebreather, and checked his wrist tracker. A dizzying variety of boat hulls slid by above him. All around, in every direction, countless anchor chains and pieces of ancient junk formed a tangled, disorienting maze. Where the heck was he? Was his wrist tracker homing in on the beacon?

Even as he squeezed and contorted his way through this labyrinth, a part of his mind pondered Roxanna's submarine. No way could a sub, even a small one, get through here. And wouldn't a sub have to surface in order to transfer the nukes on board?

Finally, Adam reached the beacon. He then located *Tad* and *Lila*'s sleek hulls. He surfaced under the overhanging bow of a boat several boats away.

*   *   *

As she neared roof level, Tripnee paused to catch her breath. Then, very slowly, with a silenced Beretta Pico in each hand, she elbowed open the door which gave onto the roof. Ah-ha. Just as she'd thought. The terrorists were indeed on high alert, covering their bases. Two sentries lay prone at the edge of the roof. Each with his head poking over the lip, looking down on the marina with night-vision goggles. Each with an AK-47 at his side.

One of the men, sensing motion behind him, turned, bringing up his rifle. Without hesitation, Tripnee put a bullet in his head, and another in the head of the man beside him. *Psst,*

psst. Then, pro that she was, she put a second slug in each skull. *Psst, psst.*

Rapidly, she chained the door shut she'd just come through and dragged the two bodies around behind a brick chimney. This done, she laid out and assembled her M82, and, instead of the spot occupied by the terrorists, she took up an even better position, one overlooking not only the entire harbor but also a broad swath of the sea outside the harbor.

* * *

"I'm in position," Adam's voice crackled quietly over their coms. "Thirty feet from targets. What's everyone's status?"

"I'm also in position," Tripnee reported. "They had two snipers up here. Both now dead. These perps are on high alert."

"Good going," Adam whispered. "Are you okay?"

"Doing fine. Although I could use a sherpa to carry my rifle."

Sophia's voice rattled through the static, "These guys really are on alert. They've got sentries everywhere. It's as though they expect us. Tripnee, I'll fly drones up to watch your back. Adam, be careful."

"What's going on aboard *Tad* and *Lila?*" Adam whispered.

"They're pretending to party. Trying to maintain their cover. But even from here they look totally lame. The fact is they're jumpy and constantly looking around."

"Hmmm. Any portholes or hatches open?"

"None."

"Empty cabins?"

"As far as I can tell, none."

"Where are the sentries?"

"All over the place," Sophia answered. "Above and below

deck on all three boats. And on neighboring boats. Judging from the bulges under their clothes, they're heavily armed."

"They're expecting something."

"Or just taking no chances with their last remaining nukes."

"Something's fishy."

"Something's definitely not right."

CHAPTER 30

CHAPTER 30

IDRA HARBOR

O *kay, things are dicey. Nothing new about that.*
Adam's cans of knockout gas weren't going to be of much use. And the old sneak aboard and shoot 'em one-by-one wasn't going to work either. Well, it just so happened that he still had a few tricks up his sleeve, a few little game-changing gifts to deliver.

Adam submerged with as much stealth as he could muster, dropped to the harbor floor, inched along the junky bottom, and then rose straight up directly beneath the 80-foot terrorist karavoskara, *Tad*, formerly the *Al-Gazi*. Floating with his face inches from the hull, thankful his rebreather emitted no bubbles to give away his presence, he pulled out an improvised explosive device the size of a paperback thriller novel. Fanatical Islamists weren't the only ones who knew how to use these babies. He peeled off the plastic backing sheet to expose soft stickum and pressed the IED onto the hull. He figured three would do the job, one near the bow, another amidships, a third near the stern. Then he repeated the process, placing three more bombs along the hull of *Lila*, formerly *The Crescent Moon*. Nice, beautiful, sweet, good little bombs. Just right for sinking boats without harming the neighbors.

Adam then worked his way out from under the harbor flotilla and swam underwater around to the mega yacht, *Galel*, outside the mole. Using much bigger charges, he spaced four bombs along the bottom of its broad, 150-foot-long hull.

As he stuck the last IED in place, what do you know? He found himself looking at the underside of a small submarine about 35-feet in length fitted into an underwater indentation scooped from the bottom of the mega yacht. Hidden from the surface, this submarine bay would allow the sub to come and go undetected. Unbelievable. Since when did a bunch of terrorists have equipment like this? Yet there it was, as big as life within arm's reach, faintly glowing in his underwater night-vision goggles.

He reached deep into his fanny pack and drew out two more IEDs and stuck them onto the sub. Then he pulled out a can of underwater super-sticky expanding foam. Taking care not to miss a single one, he swam around and plugged all the through-hull ports—the intakes and exhausts—of both the sub and its mother ship, thereby shutting off all engine cooling: with no water circulation to cool them, the ship and sub engines would rapidly overheat and seize up. Neither *Galel* nor the sub would be motoring very far anytime soon.

Adam swam underwater back into and across the harbor and pulled himself into the skiff. He peeled off his swim gear, toweled off, and pulled on bulletproof armor—then arrayed himself again in the blond wig and loose, goofy sailor outfit. Next, after checking in with and getting a green light from Tripnee and Sophia, he put on a backpack and grabbed a very special duffle, both heavy. Then he sauntered out along the mole back to the 65-foot ketch, *Patriot,* whose owners had been so friendly.

CHAPTER 31

CHAPTER 31

PATRIOT

Adam had a good feeling about these people, whose names turned out to be Dave and Marge. Adam asked if the three of them could go below and have a private conversation. Figuring the best way to win their cooperation was to be completely open, Adam outlined the situation, emphasized what was at stake, and then made them an offer.

"With your permission, I'd like to rent your boat for one night, tonight. Starting right now."

He plopped the duffle bag on the salon table, opened its lengthwise zipper and revealed bundle upon bundle of hundred-dollar bills. The thing was chock full of bundles.

"There's a million and a half dollars in this bag. More than enough to cover any damage. And it'll even buy you an entire new boat or two if it should come to that. I'll do my best to keep the damage to a minimum. Regardless of what happens, the money's yours to keep for the one night's rent. I'm asking this of you—and making this offer—because millions of lives are at stake. What do you say?"

There was a reason Adam had had a good feeling about this sweet couple. Their response was heart-warming. Dave and Marge talked quietly for a while, then, as Marge stood beside him, tearing up, trembling but trying to look brave, Dave turned to Adam, and said, "How about I stay with you? I think you're going to need some backup. I don't look like much, but I was a grunt in 'Nam."

"That's one beautiful offer, Dave. But my team and I have a plan, and the best thing right now is for you and Marge to take this money, leave right now and go check into a resort away from here, maybe the one on Mandraki Bay. And, by the way, you look great."

Marge let out a huge sigh, wiping away tears.

If these were the sort of people he, Tripnee, and Sophia were struggling to save from nuclear annihilation, they were clearly worth it. And failure was not an option.

While music, laughter, and yelling spilled out from various parties around the marina, Adam relaxed in the cockpit of *Patriot*, giving Dave and Marge time to exit the area. So far so good. Dave and Marge's boat was directly between *Tad* and *Lila*, which were in the center of the harbor flotilla, and *Galel*, which was moored outside the mole. Anyone going from *Tad* or *Lila* toward *Galel*, especially if they were in a hurry, was likely to cross *Patriot*'s deck or a boat nearby.

Patriot had a central cockpit nestled between cabins fore and aft, creating a foxhole feeling. Adam stood on the companionway steps, his head just showing, a fully loaded, silenced Glock in each hand, and peered through a multi-boat thicket of masts, dodgers, and rigging toward *Tad* and *Lila*. Soon, he hoped, these two boats were going down. But not fast. Not all at once. They needed to sink slowly. Slowly enough for the terrorists to have time—if the nukes were on board—to grab them and bring them this way toward *Patriot*.

He pulled out the IED remote detonator, punched in a password and awakened the device. There's an understood rule in chess that says: Whenever possible, force your opponent to move in ways that disrupt his plans and benefit you. So, how about a series of boat sinkings to flush out the nukes? *Let's see what plays out on this real-life chessboard.*

Adam pushed a button. Then another. A distinct but muffled denotation on *Tad* and one on *Lila* rumbled through the night, cutting through the marina music and party chatter. Soon the music stopped. Then yelling and screaming spread through the flotilla.

"There's definitely commotion," Sophia said over his earpiece. "They're scrambling to figure out what hit 'em."

Time to up the pressure. Adam hit two more buttons, and heard two more muffled explosions.

"Both boats are taking on water," Sophia said. "This is beautiful. Adam, you're a genius."

"Watch that," Tripnee said. "He's my genius."

"Focus," Adam said. "Focus."

Time to finish them off. Adam set off the third IED on each boat. Two more distinct explosions, but sounding even more muffled, no doubt because both boats were already knee-deep or maybe waist-deep in sea water.

"Roxanna's coming up out of *Tad*," Sophia said. "She's got a nuke and an Uzi and is wearing body armor. And now she has three people around her with AK-47s."

"Whoa. A guy just popped up out of *Lila*. It's Aziz. With a nuke. Interesting, he's handing off the nuke to big-shouldered Sahiba."

Adam saw movement through the forest of masts and shrouds, but couldn't make out details.

"Roxanna and Sahiba with nukes. Surrounded by guys with AK-47s. Headed your way."

Adam saw them coming. A tight phalanx of armed men all moving as a unit. How did they get organized so fast?

Moving across the sailboats, each terrorist had to do a fair amount of dodging around and over boat railings, shrouds, boat paraphernalia, and drunken sailors. But overall, they moved in unison as a group. If Adam started shooting and they returned fire together en masse, he wouldn't last five seconds.

Then heads started popping. Bodies dropped. The group's tight organization—the very fact they moved in formation—set them apart, separated them from the surrounding dazed and boozed-up civilians. This allowed Tripnee to identify them and blow their heads off one-by-one.

What a great girlfriend.

Adam's two Glocks also opened up, dropping one, two, three. As heads exploded, one startled bystander downwind and down range of a suddenly headless terrorist found herself splattered from eye level to knee level in a fine spray of bone, tissue, and blood.

As heads continued to explode, the phalanx faltered. After six or seven terrorists dropped in their tracks, it dawned on the others that being in this formation was hazardous to their health. So, the phalanx broke up, its members scattering.

Abandoned, the small, wiry Roxanna screamed with rage. Exposed, she and Sahiba, who was big but nimble, moved even faster, dodging, jumping, running, leaping—all while gripping their heavy nuclear suitcases.

As soon as Adam caught sight of Roxanna, he whipped a Glock toward her. High time to put this one down once and for all. In the split second before he released a bullet, an oblivious sailor bumbled into his line of fire. This poor guy, a minute later, got slammed by big Sahiba, pitching him into the water.

Okay, then. Seizing the moment, Adam put a slug into Sahiba's broad forehead. Then he scanned for Roxanna. Where was she? There. Ducking down to grab Sahiba's nuke. Again, Adam swung the gun toward her, zeroing in, tension already on the trigger.

But at that instant, bullets hit Adam from behind. Down, down, down he went, and almost out. Reeling and disoriented, he struggled to his feet and looked back. Three men on the stern deck of *Galel* blasted away with AK-47s—two firing at him, the other up at Tripnee. Thank God, he and Tripnee wore body armor.

CHAPTER 32

GALEL

A dam ducked down and grabbed his remote-controller. Time to put an end to this bullshit. He jabbed a series of buttons. Instantly, explosions ripped the air. *Kaboom. Kaboom. Kaboom. Kaboom. Galel* jumped and shook. Then settled deeper and deeper into the water. *Galel* and its sub were going down fast.

Now Roxanna and her crew would have no place to go and would be caught out in a crossfire. He and Tripnee could cut them down and recover those precious, deadly, diabolical weapons. Well, at least that was the plan.

But even as *Galel*'s crew clambered off its gangplank fleeing their sinking ship, Roxanna slipped past them and ran forward along the deck, which was nearly awash.

*   *   *

The hail of bullets coming up from *Galel* forced Tripnee to duck and stay down. Then came the beautiful explosions. Adam sure knew how to blow things up. What a boyfriend.

Tripnee risked peering over the roof's edge, sighting through her M82's powerful night-vision scope. Far below, everything was moving in a blur. Roxanna ran through deepening water and jumped into a small powerboat mounted on the bow deck of *Galel*. The next moment, the bow of *Galel* disappeared below the waves, and the powerboat floated free and raced away.

"Adam," Tripnee yelled into their earpiece coms, "that Roxanna bitch just launched a speedboat off the bow of *Galel.*"

Right then, talk about amazing, a hundred yards out from the mole, what the fuck. There, breaching the surface, was a real submarine. Not a miniature sub. But an actual, World War II-style military submarine. The conning tower was already out of the water, and the long, sleek, black hull—maybe a hundred-and-twenty feet long—was coming into view, water pouring off it. Roxanna powered around to the far side of the conning tower, taking cover where Tripnee couldn't get off a shot.

"Fuck shit hell!" Tripnee yelled into her com. "Are you seeing this, they've got a real, actual submarine."

CHAPTER 33

MOHAMMAD

The hatch on the sub's tower opened. Two suitcases, no doubt the nukes, flew smoothly up from the far side and disappeared down the hatch like basketballs dropping into a net. A man's head and torso came up out of the hatch, and Tripnee blew the guy's noggin to smithereens. Almost simultaneously, or a nano second later, in a complete blur, the tiny, lithe body of Roxanna slid in a flash down the opening on the far side of the headless torso.

Immediately, the submarine began to dive. Tripnee blasted away at the conning tower. The M82 was famous for destroying trucks, airplanes, and even light tanks. But her bullets bounced off the thick steel.

"No, no, no, no. They're getting away."

*   *   *

The instant Tripnee mentioned the speedboat, Adam raced back along the mole and jumped into the skiff. Firing up the motor, he cut across the harbor and executed a roaring fast turn out through the exit.

He was just in time to see the long, dark hull of the sub slide below the waves. For a while the conning tower was still visible, but even as he caught up with it, that too disappeared below the surface.

This couldn't be happening. Frantic, beside himself, he gunned the outboard, racing to get ahead of the sub. As the light skiff planed and skipped across the waves, he tore off his loose jacket and body armor, pulled on fins, mask, and rebreather, and grabbed his fanny pack.

Hoping to God he'd judged the spot correctly, he killed the engine and threw himself into the water. Swimming straight down deep, he felt the big sub coming on fast, pushing water out of its path. The sub's pressure wave pushed him to the side.

In a desperate frenzy, he kicked and stroked with all he had. But the long, massive, sleek shape slid by out of reach, picking up speed. Try as he might, he couldn't get to it. Soon he was spent, exhausted, done for.

But he kept on kicking, stroking, drawing on he didn't-know-what. From somewhere, from outside himself, from deep within, he found some kind of wellspring—he had no idea how or what—but he kept on—and kept on—kicking and stroking—-kicking and stroking.

Finally, he got close enough to stretch out and touch the machine. But it was moving too fast, and there was nothing to grip. The monster was slipping by, about to get away. Then, his extended fingertips found a handhold on the very stern of the sub, a raised nameplate showing the name: *Mohammad.*

But the thing was moving too fast. He gripped it anyway, and instantly regretted it, as his arm felt ripped from its socket. Like a Raggedy Ann doll with an arm tied to a clothesline in a hurricane, he was stretched out, blasted, raked and pummeled.

But no way could he let go. If his arm, his wrist, his shoulder pulled away, so fucking what? *Just let me hold on this one last time. Then you can have the hand, the arm.* If he could just pull off this one last thing, a one-armed future was doable.

He reached into his fanny pack with his other hand, pulled out a super-sized IED, tore off the plastic backing with his teeth and slapped it onto the sub. Then, just as his grip finally failed, he slapped on another.

As the sub tore away into the depths, Adam surfaced, then swam to and pulled himself into the skiff. Digging frantically for the remote-controller, he tapped in the password and set off the two bombs. The shockwave sent an eruption of water skyward a quarter mile away. Do you suppose that sub was having a little trouble with its ass end blown off?

Adam motored out to the site where giant bubbles were still coming up. Nursing his arm, he put out a sea anchor to hold the skiff in place, then pulled on his swim gear and the rebreather. He took his time, looked around. What a lovely night it was. Funny how he'd never before so fully appreciated the sheer beauty of a twenty-knot *meltemi*.

The whole rear of the sub was gone. Adam swam into the gaping opening. His infrared headlamp and night vision revealed body after body with startled, terrified expressions. The crew hadn't closed the inner hatches separating the sub's different chambers. Probably not the most experienced of submariners.

His internal alarm system began to sound as he neared the bow. Where were the nukes? And, for that matter, where was Roxanna? Working his way back to the middle of the sub, he looked up into the conning tower. What the hell? The hatch had been opened, and he saw someone swimming up toward the surface.

Swimming up as fast as he could, Adam surfaced in time to see Roxanna pulling herself aboard his skiff.

She fired up the engine, pulled in the sea anchor and accelerated out to sea. Fifty yards away, Adam could only watch. This damned jihadi just wouldn't give up and couldn't, wouldn't be stopped. And there, right there!, she was racing off into the distance. Looking around, there was nothing he could do.

He'd never felt so desolate or fucking helpless.

A distant pop.

Adam sensed rather than saw something change in the skiff. Roxanna must've taken her hand off the throttle, because the boat slowed to a standstill. Then it was clear: Dear blessed Tripnee had blown Roxanna's head off.

The skiff bobbed in the waves directly upwind. The wonderful waves and the fabulous *meltemi* pushed the tiny boat, with engine still idling, down to where Adam treaded water.

There was Roxanna dead as a fucking doornail still clutching the two suitcase nukes. As Adam motored back into Idra's harbor, he heard the sounds of the ongoing, perpetual boat party picking up, accelerating back into full swing, back to normal.

CHAPTER 34

CYCLOPS: PURITY

"**B**lessed are the Believers… who restrain their carnal desires… These are the heirs of Paradise…."
—Qur'an, Surah 23:1-5.

Our soldiers of Allah must be pure, devout, worthy to be the true hands of Allah. We had many sinners and people with flaws and problems. Such as way too much ambition, but I won't get started about that bitch, Roxanna.

So, we needed to get rid of sin, rottenness, unworthiness. What better way than have infidels do it.

In many ways, these Americans are diabolical and clever. But fundamentally they are like children, guileless and predictable. Yes, they have placed obstacles in our path, but we have done our research and have outplayed them. Our plan unfolds beautifully.

Allahu Akbar.

CHAPTER 35

THE SARONIC GULF

ream Voyager flaunted her beautiful self in a fair breeze, gliding northward across the Saronic Gulf. It was a world-changing accomplishment. Against all odds, the three of them had recovered thirteen suitcase nukes which they'd soon turn over to Admiral Jeppesen in Athens. As the three of them relaxed in the cockpit, relief shined on their faces, in how they sat, in their smallest gesture. Euphoria danced and twirled in the warm air.

"Can you believe it?" Sophia said. "We just brought down one hell of a lot of bad jihadis. Those guys were no match for us."

They all grinned, glowing, nodding.

After a while, Adam said, "Something I just don't understand. How can terrorists be so determined to kill millions of civilians?"

"The answer to that," Sophia said, "goes back centuries."

"So true," Tripnee said, "from its very beginning in the seventh century, Islam has been part religion, part political doctrine."

"Political doctrine?" Adam asked.

"Yeah, *Shari'a* law is essentially political," Tripnee said. "The entire Mediterranean used to be Christian, until the Muslims came out of the Arabian Peninsula and conquered it in the seventh century, installing Islam and *Shari'a* law at the point of a sword. Called it holy war, jihad, for Allah."

"*Shari'a* law," Adam said, shaking his head. "I don't get it. How can the penalty for leaving Islam, or any religion, be death? That's essentially saying no one has the right to make up his own mind, to make his own choices, or even to think his own thoughts."

Jumping up, arms akimbo, feet wide apart, hands clenched, Tripnee looked fierce as only she could. "Yeah, and how can anyone think men can beat their wives, or that a man's testimony is worth twice that of a woman?"

Adam nodded. It was nuts.

"*Shari'a*," Tripnee continued, looking askance at Sophia, "doesn't allow the basic freedoms that underlay Western civilization: I'm talking freedom of thought, speech, religion."

At that moment, far ahead on the northern horizon, the Parthenon came into view on the Acropolis high above Athens.

"In the West, our very DNA is to seek compromise, collaboration, tolerance. But the *Shari'a* forbids these things. *Shari'a* law is absolute. Every law came from the Qur'an—which Muslims regard as the express word of God and not a word can be changed, so neither can the law. We have to face the fact that the *Shari'a*, political Islam, is not compatible with democracy," Tripnee went on, helping Adam understand.

"The West has problems," Sophia said.

"We've got to defend our values," Adam said.

"So true," Tripnee said. "But one of our problems is that the minute anyone—especially, these days, if you're a white man—criticizes Islam's political doctrine, you're immediately labeled a bigot."

"Good point. I'm impressed to hear you say that," Adam said.

"Some would say this conversation is Islamophobic," Sophia said.

"But that's nuts," Tripnee said. "The principles of Western civilization are not a suicide pact. If Western culture is to survive, especially in Europe, we have to come to grips with the fact that political Islam, the political doctrine of *Shari'a*: that all the world is to be Islamic and worship Allah and jihad must be fought until that time, is incompatible with the West."

"This is a conversation more people need to have," Adam said.

At that moment, Adam noticed a small aircraft, a mere dot in the sky, pass far overhead, going from south to north toward Athens, just as they were. Was it the same airplane they'd seen en route to Folegandros? Like that plane, this one made a big circle around *Dream Voyager* before continuing on its way. Something about it troubled him, but he made no mention of it. The last thing they needed was more stress and worry.

"Well, on a positive note," Sophia said, "there's lots of diversity among Muslims. I know for a fact that many ignore jihad and *taqiyya*--that idea that all Muslims have to lie to non-Muslims--and only want to make their prayers. Do you know that in Iran, which is Shi'a, fewer than four percent of the people are religious? Over sixty percent dance and drink—and stop only during the holy month of Ramadan, the celebration when Allah sent down the Qur'an to his people."

Tripnee tossed her head defiantly, and said, "Yeah, and that four percent is made up of the Iranian Revolutionary Guard Corps and the mad mullahs who want to nuke the world to bring back the Mahdi, who'll bring on the end of the world. And, surveys show, that a majority of the one point six billion Muslims worldwide favor the imposition of *Shari'a* law on the whole world."

CHAPTER 36

ATHENS

Twelve black Suburbans lined up on the Kalamaki quay made quite a display visible from a long way off. As *Dream Voyager* dropped its sails, motored in and Med-moored, Adam was reassured to see his old Navy SEAL buddy Admiral Ty Jeppesen waving back at him.

It was also good to see fifty or so alert, heavily armed US Marines fanned out along the quay.

Jeppesen climbed aboard, beaming, looking happier than Adam had ever seen him. Uncharacteristic of the usually reserved guy, Jeppesen pulled Adam into a hug. Addressing the three of them, he said, "Well done. Well done."

Seeing their bandages, Jeppesen asked about their wounds. When they reassured him they were okay—and especially when he saw that, although obviously stiff and sore, they nonetheless moved with an irrepressible joy—his celebratory mood returned.

Spreading his arms wide, grinning from ear-to-ear, he said, "Thank you so, so much. The three of you pulled off Mission Impossible."

Tripnee smiled, then, frowning, said, "The sooner we get these bombs off the boat, the better."

Jeppesen signaled for a squad of Marines to come onboard. Adam told them where to find the bombs, and they bounded down the companionway to get them.

"The three of you deserve a slew of medals and a parade down Fifth Avenue," Jeppesen said. "Unfortunately, black ops have to stay secret, so we can't do a public ceremony. But the president wants to thank all three of you in person in the White House."

Tripnee frowned. "That's a nice offer, but I'd prefer that Adam and I just keep sailing."

Jeppesen looked surprised. "You literally saved millions of lives and prevented World War III. It'll be private, but we're talking about a full-blown, pull-out-all-the-stops ceremony in the White House with the President of the United States. A very, very grateful president."

Then, turning to Adam, Jeppesen continued, "You know the president. After what you did in the San Francisco Bay Area, he considers you a national hero and a special friend. Hell, it's public knowledge that you're good friends. You had to know he'd insist on thanking you himself in person." Then, almost pleading, he said, "And I'll be honest, if I don't get you to come, I'll never hear the end of it."

As longtime buddies, Adam and Ty Jeppesen had an intuitive way of communicating. With a nod and a look, Adam let Ty know that in private he would talk with Tripnee, address her concerns, and work things out so that, most likely, they'd all be accepting the president's invitation.

They were interrupted by the Marines coming up from below. Four carried two bombs each, while the others, including a major, carried one. As his men filed off *Dream Voyager*, the major conferred with the admiral, then turned to thank the trio and shake their hands. As he climbed the gangplank to the quay, he said, "The sooner we secure these bombs the better."

"Amen to that," they all said.

The nine men, along with the forty or so other Marines, piled into the twelve Suburbans and drove away, leaving the quay empty.

"Where's your vehicle?" Adam asked Ty.

"Oh. I'm using a ten-year-old Ford from the embassy motor pool. It's up that way." Ty waved toward where the quay met land.

"It's just like you to keep a ridiculously low profile," Adam said. "You know, old buddy, in case you hadn't realized it, you're a big cheese. You should treat yourself to some creature comforts and a little more security. Speaking of which, you do at least have a security detail, right?"

"Oh, I've got my assistant, George. He's taking a nap in the car. George's putting his younger brother through college and stays up most nights creating websites and doesn't get much sleep. So, I'm happy to give him a break whenever I can."

"That's crazy, old buddy," Adam said, looking fondly at his old friend. Realizing they hadn't been formally introduced, Adam said, "Where are my manners?" then introduced the admiral and Sophia.

"This calls for a toast," Jeppesen said. "By a stroke of amazing good luck, look what I happen to have." With a flourish, he pulled a chilled, magnum-sized bottle of champagne from an insulated shoulder bag.

Sophia excused herself. "I'll be right back."

With the three of them alone in the cockpit, Tripnee whispered, "Going to the White House sounds great, but there's something about that bitch. Does she have to come?"

"The thing is," Adam said, "we couldn't have pulled this off without her."

They brought up glasses and popped open the bubbly, which Adam recognized as very fine indeed.

At that moment, Sophia reappeared looking dolled up and gorgeous, and rejoined them at the cockpit table.

Intending to fill the glasses, Ty lifted the magnum—and it exploded.

Bang, bang. Bang, bang, bang. Bang, bang.

The four dove for the deck. Adam risked a quick look to see a wild scene unfolding in the parking area at the head of the quay. A panel truck accelerated away, tires squealing, as a man in a Marine uniform—it had to be George, Jeppesen's aide—blasted away with a handgun.

"I think George just saved our lives," Adam said.

"He definitely saved mine," Sophia said. "That shot was aimed straight at me. If that bottle hadn't been in the way, I'd be toast."

Indeed, they'd all been sprayed by champagne and shattered glass. But amazingly, the thick, full bottle had stopped or deflected the bullet, leaving Sophia unhurt.

Greek police arrived and secured the scene. Afterward, the four of them talked with George aboard *Dream Voyager*.

"Something about that panel van wasn't right," George said. "But it was parked a ways away from me, and I didn't think much of it. The instant I heard the shot, though, I knew it'd come from the van. I fired back immediately."

"And thank God you did, son," Jeppesen said. "Very good work."

"You kept them from getting off more shots," Adam said, "Very quick thinking."

"You really were very brave," Tripnee said. "You took 'em on with just a pistol, out in the open."

"But for you, George, I'd be dead," Sophia gushed, giving his arm a squeeze. "And I'd just changed out of my bulletproof vest."

The young man, a Navy lieutenant, looked dazzled. Sophia had that effect on people, or to be more precise, on men.

"I've been studying jihadi tactics for a long time," Jeppesen said. "Somehow that didn't seem like a jihadi hit. Not their style. But who else could it be?"

"Well, one thing for sure, things are still hot around here," Sophia said. "All the more reason for all of us to go right away to the White House."

Jeppesen looked thoughtful. "That shot was aimed directly at you, Sophia."

"That's not the first time that's happened," Adam said.

"These terrorists seem hell-bent on killing you, in particular," Jeppesen said to Sophia. "I have an idea. One way to protect you is to make them think this attack was successful."

"How?" Tripnee asked.

"We let it be known that Sophia is dead," Jeppesen said. "From time to time, we have to do things like this. I'll have our Athens station chief provide a body to create a traceable record, an official death certificate. Then I'll put out the word so it gets to Cyclops."

"Beautiful," Adam said. "That, combined with Sophia disappearing, will take the target off her back."

Sophia smiled coyly and did a girlish twirl on her tiptoes. "I've always wanted to go to America."

CHAPTER 37

THE OVAL OFFICE

Their CIA jet landed at Andrews Joint Military Base outside Washington, DC and taxied over to a long, black limousine and two black government SUVs, all with men in suits standing at attention beside them. Stairs were quickly rolled into place. As they filed off the jet, a driver held the limo door open for them. With a welcoming wave and a slight bow, he indicated they should all climb in, which they did, finding it spacious and comfortable.

Sophia laughed with delight. "Such luxury."

George remarked, "Wow, this is the Beast, the president's personal limo. The admiral and I have never gotten this treatment before. You three rate."

"Creature comforts," Tripnee said, looking at Adam, "are nice, especially for our walking wounded."

As they were driven through morning traffic into DC, Jeppesen took an urgent call. A few minutes later, putting away his phone and looking grim, he said, "It's damned lucky you finished rounding up those nukes and that we're getting back now. The NSA is picking up chatter from multiple sources that a terrorist attack on the United States is imminent. If the reports are to be believed, one—or possibly more—major terrorist honchos just arrived right here in DC." Looking out the limo windows at the Lincoln Memorial, the Washington Monument, and the Capitol Building beyond, he shook his head. "The threat level is through the roof."

Adam winced. "How can we help?"

Before Jeppesen could answer, his phone rang again. When he put away his phone a second time, he said, "That was the White House. The president wants us to join him in the Oval Office for a quick initial thank you. And then for this evening, he's rearranged his schedule for us to have that pull-out-the-stops private ceremony."

They entered the White House through a lesser-used side door. Jeppesen, as one the president's key national security advisors, and George, as his aide, were well known at the White House and were ushered straight through.

Adam, Tripnee, and Sophia, on the other hand, underwent a thorough Secret Service security scan, pat-down and pelvic area X-ray. Made sense. In this day and age, body cavities had to be checked. *Be glad it's not a strip search with a body-cavity hand probe.* Of course, they had to turn over their weapons—including Tripnee, who now carried her M82 everywhere. Maybe the search was excessive. But it made sense to take zero chances, especially with a terrorist attack expected at any moment.

Their Oval Office meeting was brief, but—*let's be honest*—amazing. After all, this was the President of the United States and the leader of the free world. The man had taken the time to learn the details of each of their exploits, including even those of Lieutenant George. As he warmly chatted up each of them, the president specifically praised key contributions of each and poured on heartfelt thanks.

When one of the president's aides caught his eye and cleared his throat, it was time for the meeting to end.

Sophia, evidently mustering her courage, spoke up, "Mr. President, it's an incredible thrill to meet you. I've always been a security buff and this is the most secure building in the world. It would be a dream come true if I could have a behind-the-scenes tour."

A Secret Service guy, who stayed in the background but was never more than a few feet from the president, said, "I'm afraid that's impossible."

"By the way, everyone," said the President, "this is Bob, the head of my security detail today." Then, turning to Bob, he said, "These are heroes of America. They've just repeatedly, over and over, again and again, in huge ways, risked their lives in order to protect this country and the world. If we can't trust them, who can you trust?"

George, apparently also mustering his courage, cleared his throat and said to the group, "Sophia has dedicated her career to fighting terrorism." Then, after exchanging glances with Jeppesen and getting a nod, he turned to Sophia and said, "I'd be glad to be your guide."

Wearing a thousand-watt smile, Sophia leaned in close and squeezed his arm. "Would you, George? I would love that so much."

Then she flashed that lit-up smile around the room, lingering on each of the men, and all the men stood a little taller.

After they filed out of the Oval Office, George and Sophia strolled away, her arm in his, a bounce in his step.

Jeppesen's secure phone rang. He lifted it to his ear. After a short conversation, he beckoned to Adam and Tripnee. "Our Athens bureau chief needs us on a secure video call ASAP. We're cleared to use the bunker down in the basement."

CHAPTER 38

THE WHITE HOUSE

A high-speed elevator took Adam, Tripnee, and Jeppesen deep into the White House basement.

As they approached the bunker, they passed through massive blast doors. Tripnee reflected, "Well, at least the president has this secure shelter designed to withstand even a direct nuclear strike."

"Unfortunately," Jeppesen said, "that's a myth. The fact is, it's designed to withstand anything *but* a direct nuclear hit."

Tripnee's eyes opened wide. "Sorry to hear that."

"Me, too," Jeppesen said. "I'm afraid a direct hit—even a suitcase nuke detonation inside the building—would wipe out the entire White House, including everyone in this underground bunker."

The three of them took seats facing a giant flat screen on the opposite wall. Jeppesen sat in front of a small camera so that only he would be visible.

Adam and Tripnee sat to the side, off camera.

The Athens CIA bureau chief, an African-American man with a striking resemblance to Dr. Martin Luther King, said, "We received an urgent message from a guy who says he used to be part of *Jamaat-e Aleimlaq*. He's calling from the Island of Folegandros, and he says he has information about an imminent attack."

Surprised, Adam said, "We surveilled two guys on

Folegandros, Isa Kaan, and Dogu Kubilay. Dogu was a gung-ho enforcer for Cyclops. Both seemed to have defected. Could be one of them."

Jeppesen hit a few keys on a keyboard. When a face appeared on the big screen, Adam whispered, "It's Isa Kaan."

Jeppesen introduced himself, and said, "I understand you have information about an imminent attack?"

Isa Kaan said, "You've got a big problem. I know you know about the Cyclops *jamaat*. What you don't know is that Cyclops is about to launch a major attack."

"Tell me more."

"The attack will be devastating. It will create hell on earth for generations. It will set Islam and the West on a path of open conflict that Islam can't win."

"I need details."

"They will use suitcase nuclear bombs, lots of them."

"When? Where? Who?"

"That's all I know. But you have to stop it. Or the entire world will be torn apart."

"How do you know this? Who are you?"

"Who I am is not important. I was part of what you call the Cyclopean *jamaat*, but no more. You must not tell anyone that I talked with you—no one."

"How do I know this is true? Why have you come forward?"

"I used to think jihad was noble and the best way to right the wrongs done to the Islamic world. I actually believed dying as a martyr was the guaranteed way into Paradise. But I've realized there are no circumstances on earth where violence is permissible. Violence only leads to greater harm. I've opened my eyes. Cyclops and others use jihad to justify their love of power and desire to control others. They send young people to die fighting unwinnable wars. The truth is, these leaders only cause misery."

"Good for you," Jeppesen said, nodding, "that you've realized this."

"I've come a long way."

"You have."

"We have a core problem: Islam cannot be criticized in any shape or form in the Middle East," Isa said. "But if I can open my eyes, others can as well. People drawn to jihad are not that different from everyone else. People can change."

A voice from somewhere off-screen yelled, "Isa, what are you doing?"

"That's Dogu Kubilay," Adam whispered.

BANG.

A shot rang out and Isa slumped forward, a bullet hole in his forehead. Then the screen went dead.

Jeppesen, Tripnee, and Adam sat in stunned silence.

Finally, Tripnee said, "Okay, I just can't keep it in. There's something about Sophia. I can't shake a gut feeling she's somehow involved with this."

"But where's the evidence?" Adam asked.

"Well," Tripnee said, "she keeps expressing pro-Islamic viewpoints."

"If she were a terrorist practicing *taqiyya* to fool us," Jeppesen said, "wouldn't she be more likely to condemn Islam? The very fact she doesn't hide her mildly pro-Islamic sympathies tells me she's sincere. Don't you think?"

Adam said, "She identified and played a crucial role in helping us kill dozens of terrorists. And there's just no way we could have captured those thirteen nukes without her."

"How," concluded Jeppesen, "could Sophia possibly be a terrorist?"

CHAPTER 39
CYCLOPS: ALLAHU AKBAR

T he White House defenses are formidable: a perimeter of vehicle barriers which pop up at the touch of a button, the world's most thorough security screening, Secret Service everywhere, fences, high-tech sensors galore, including super sensitive plutonium/uranium detectors, bulletproof windows, patrol dogs, and bomb-sniffing dogs, daily scans for surveillance bugs, a small but well-armed army in the basement plus nearby fighter jets and additional forces ready to deploy at a moment's notice, a nearly impregnable underground bunker system, and—what really pisses me off—the world's most advanced drone shield system guaranteed to thwart any and all drone attacks.

Merely exploding a suitcase nuke a hundred yards away won't cut it. But explode the nuke inside the building! That will cook the works—the whole sinful bunch—including everyone below ground. Now that sure sounds good.

Allah is indeed great. The idea that something so vast and powerful—America and its seat of power the White House—could be shaken and obliterated by something the size of an egg—my fake eye. Only in a universe ruled by Allah could such a thing come to pass.

The gaping hole in my head where my left eye used to be is bigger than one might think. Praise Allah—and, well, also my German grandparents who paid for it and the Swedish doctors who made it—for my prosthetic eye. My lovely, fake eye. It even tracks so closely with my right eye that almost no one notices it's artificial. Especially men, who are distracted by other things about me. You wouldn't think it possible, but it is. *Alhamdulillah*.

Inshallah, all goes well. We have rid ourselves of bad people, and along the way have had to sacrifice good people, too. Now we are cleansed, blessed, and at one with Allah. We are the humble tools of Allah, well on our way to decapitating the Great Satan. Let America crumble and collapse. Out of the chaos, Allah will bring forth a glorious caliphate according to His divine vision. Ours is not to figure this out. Ours is to submit and obey.

CHAPTER 40

THE BIG EVENT

That evening, true to his word, the president rolled out the red carpet—all with no press coverage, of course. The East Room was decked out for the occasion and even had a string quartet playing in one corner. The joint chiefs of the military, key members of Congress, and the heads of various intelligence agencies were present, as well as several members of the presidential cabinet and a number of close friends of the president—including a few famous billionaires and entertainers.

But missing were George and Sophia. Given their earlier discussion, this prompted Adam, Jeppesen, and Tripnee to exchange glances with raised eyebrows.

The evening was well underway when a dozen secret service agents burst into the room and surrounded the president. Adam, Tripnee, and Jeppesen, sitting in places of honor next to the President, heard agent Bob say, "Sir, our drone shield system was disabled a few moments ago by a small explosive. We're taking you immediately to the underground bunker."

Adam, Tripnee, and Jeppesen leapt to their feet.

Tripnee said, "This is Sophia's doing." Then, turning to the President, she said, "Mr. President, may I have your authorization to take my rifle up to the roof? This is Sophia's work. I know this bitch. She's going to fly drones—with nukes—in here to attack you."

The President looked at Bob and Adam, who both nodded.

Adam said, "Listen to her, sir."

Tripnee continued in a rush. "Let me go to the roof. I know how she thinks—how she flies drones. There's a chance I can shoot down at least some of them."

Jeppesen blurted out, "I recommend it, sir. If anyone can shoot drones down, it'd be Tripnee."

The President, who was already being hustled out of the room, yelled over his shoulder, "Do it, Tripnee. Help her, Bob; make it happen."

The room erupted into pandemonium, with people rushing to follow the President while others ran for the exits.

Tripnee, with Bob close behind, raced to get her M82. Hefting the long case, she slid her arms through the shoulder straps, and headed for the roof. The elevators were swamped with people desperate to get to the fortified bunker in the basement. So Tripnee ran up the stairs, taking two and three at a time. Bob did his best to keep up, but Tripnee moved with the grace and speed of a cheetah, and the Secret Service agent fell behind.

Tripnee flew up the final flight of stairs to the roof, to find her way blocked by a short, wide man. The guy—who was not a regular Secret Service agent but some sort of officious capital policeman on roof patrol--said, "No way. You're not taking that"—he gestured toward her gun case—"to the roof. In fact, you're not allowed to have that."

"It's an emergency. We're under attack. The president authorized me to get to the roof, *now*."

"Nope. Give me that—"

Swearing, Tripnee delivered a round house kick to the guy's head so fast he didn't know what hit him. Stepping over his unconscious body, she pushed open the door onto the roof just in time to hear the faint buzz of fast-approaching drones.

On some level, she was not surprised. She'd actually anticipated something like this, and had in her gun case night-vision goggles plus several magazines of "drone shot." Instead of a single slug, these rounds contained buckshot perfect for bringing down Sophia's damned quadracopters.

As the sound of the drones grew louder and louder, she realized she faced an entire swarm. Maybe a dozen? Or, oh-oh, more likely several dozen. And by the sound, many weren't so small. Well, the bigger they come, the easier to see and hit. Or so she hoped.

With practiced speed, she assembled and loaded her weapon and whipped on night vision. And in the nick of time—or was she too late? She had just lifted her rifle when a first wave of drones swarmed in low and attached themselves to bulletproof windows below her rooftop position.

Ka-blaam, ka-blaam, ka-blaam, ka-blaam.

Not good. These lead drones had blown open a bunch of windows, clearing the way for bigger drones to swoop into the building with the real bombs. This was definitely Sophia's work. It reeked of the termagant. It was just how the slut would do things.

A second wave of bigger drones streamed in. Large enough to carry nuclear bombs. Balancing her gun on the waist-high perimeter wall at the roof edge, Tripnee began blasting away. Each shot sent forth a pattern of buckshot perfect for decimating the lethal buggers. Bam, bam, bam, bam.

These were nukes, all right. Her buckshot not only destroyed the drones, it also did a nice job of rendering the nukes inoperable. One, two, three dropped out of the night air.

But there were too many. She wasn't going to get them all. If even one got inside the building, God help the world.

CHAPTER 41

DUPONT CIRCLE

Meanwhile, the moment they heard that the drone shield had been disabled, Adam and Jeppesen knew what they had to do. Fortunately, they'd sensed there was indeed something suspicious about Sophia. Jeppesen had told George to slip a tracker—a tiny device that looked exactly like a dime—into Sophia's pocket. George had protested, but had followed orders.

Adam and Jeppesen raced from the East Room, charged out of the building and jumped into Jeppesen's government SUV. The Admiral opened his laptop and hit a few keys. Sure enough, the tracker showed up on the screen two miles away. Adam already had the vehicle in motion. They roared away from the White House and in moments were barreling though the streets of DC.

"Let's see if we can take her by surprise," Adam said. "Better chance of grabbing her before she sets off any nukes."

Jeppesen relayed directions, glancing back and forth between his tracking screen and the scene before them. Checking his watch, he saw that it was less than two minutes since they'd left the White House. He pulled two Glock pistols from the glove box, handed one to Adam, and said, "She's around the next corner to the right, in the middle of the block."

But before they reached the corner, the tracker showed Sophia moving. Fast.

"Oh-oh, she's moving."

When they reached the corner, they caught a glimpse of a white windowless van careening around a far corner.

"Do you suppose she got her drones inside the White House and has 'em on timers to give her time to get completely out of the fallout zone?" Adam asked.

"Interesting. She's happy to send other people to their death, but when it's time for her to make the big sacrifice, she attacks remotely."

"Old buddy," Jeppesen said, sweat pouring off his forehead, "this can't be how this ends."

"If I know anything," Adam said, "you and me, we'll give it our all. But we're going to need a little help from the big guy upstairs."

Jeppesen shouted directions while Adam pushed their powerful vehicle up to and beyond its limits, flooring it with engine screaming on the straightaways, practically rolling over with tires screeching on the turns.

They raced ahead of Sophia on a parallel boulevard, and were about to cut over and block her, when she changed direction. Again, they raced to get ahead of her, but again she veered away.

"It's as though she knows where we are," Jeppesen said in exasperation.

"Of course," exclaimed Adam. "Knowing her, she's got a drone aboard this vehicle."

Jeppesen began searching around the dash, under the front seats. Climbing into the back, he checked nooks and crevices, under the seats, everywhere. "Ha *ha*! Here it is."

Jeppesen put the tiny whirligig on the console between the front seats. Gripping the barrel of his Glock, he slammed the butt down on the mechanical insect, smashing it into a fine dust of microbits.

About the same time, the signal from the tracker in Sophia's vehicle went dead.

"Knowing her," Adam said, "she's destroyed our tracking device as well."

"Time to call in the cavalry," Jeppesen said. Getting out his secure phone, he put out a top priority all-points bulletin on Sophia's vehicle with its description and last known location and direction. Immediately, the night reverberated with the wail of dozens of sirens converging on their vicinity.

Jeppesen patched the police channel over the vehicle's speakers. A patrol car reported seeing Sophia's van and was giving chase. Others responded and set up a perimeter of roadblocks, hemming the terrorist in, cutting off escape.

Moments later, the police channel reported Sophia's vehicle had been surrounded by cop cars in the middle of an intersection in Dupont Circle, a fashionable district packed with upscale restaurants, embassies, homes, and apartments.

His phone patched into the police channel, Jeppesen ordered, "Maintain the perimeter. Keep 'em blocked in. But stay put, take cover, and do not approach the vehicle."

As Adam drove like a madman to get there, they listened as an officer narrated events: "A side door in the white van just opened. A drone just flew out. Another one. Three, four, a bunch of drones are pouring out of the white van. The drones are spreading out. It looks like, yes, it looks like one drone is landing on the roof of each squad car."

Jeppesen yelled over the police channel, "It's a trap! Get away from those drones! Get away from those vehicles!"

Ka-blaaam, ka-blaaam, KABOOM, KABOOM, KABOOM.

The explosions ripped through the Washington DC summer night.

"Oh, my God. Oh, my God," came the officer's voice. "Every squad car is a fireball."

At that moment, Adam and Jeppesen wheeled into view, and came to a stop a hundred yards from Sophia's van.

"Stay back," Jeppesen repeated over the police band, "Stay back."

Adam and Jeppesen, Glocks out, taking advantage of what cover there was, ran crouching toward the white van. Something wasn't right. Motioning Jeppesen to stay back, Adam crept to the open side door and peered in. The van appeared to be empty. Without going in or touching anything, Adam carefully studied the vehicle. Gradually, in the dim illumination provided by nearby street lamps and burning squad cars, he detected telltale traces of wires—and more. The van had no one in it. It was an autonomous, driverless, drone vehicle. And it was rigged to explode the moment anyone touched it.

So where in hell was Sophia?

CHAPTER 42

THE WASHINGTON MONUMENT

"I've got an idea," Jeppesen said. "The FCC has used an old technology called RDF—radio direction finding—since before World War II to bust pirate broadcasters whose signals interfere with licensed stations. FCC trucks might be able to get some directional fixes on Sophia's signals. We could triangulate her position with that telemetry data."

Jeppesen got on the phone and lit a fire under some FCC bureaucrats to get the ball rolling. Not just rolling, but flying. Meanwhile, Adam drove them to a secret CIA staging facility at a small private airport on the outskirts of DC.

*   *   *

Back at the edge of the White House roof, Bob and four other Secret Service agents with night vision and high-capacity shotguns came up beside Tripnee. All six blasted away at the swarming drones. The wily buggers seemed to have built-in evasion tech. But the withering rate of fire was enough to stop the onslaught. Soon the whirr of incoming drones was no more. The swarm, every last drone, had been smashed to bits without any getting inside the building. So far so good. But would more be coming?

*　　　　*　　　　*

Jeppesen bounced up and down. "Ha! The FCC vans with large antennas are picking up directional data on Sophia's low-frequency, long-wavelength radio signals."

Bringing out a map of Washington DC, he and Adam pinpointed three truck locations and, using the directional data, plotted a line from each. The lines all crossed right on the Washington Monument.

Also, the angle of the readings indicated the signals were coming from the top of the monument.

"Just like an al Qaeda terrorist to pick an iconic location dear to America," Jeppesen said.

"Also very strategic," Adam said. "An ideal place to orchestrate attacks on a whole slew of major targets. Not to mention, pretty much unassailable."

"Yeah, we can't very well just blow it up with a cruise missile."

"It's not like you to limit yourself like that," Adam said, poking his old foxhole buddy. "Plus, we've got to find out how many nukes she's got and where they're located."

The two of them planned an assault on the nearest thing to sacred ground in America, the 555-foot-tall sheer spire, the Washington Monument.

Jeppesen rapidly fine-tuned the overall arrangements, while Adam pulled on full black ops tactical gear. This included body armor, head-to-toe black clothing, soft soled, no-slip, no-sound shoes, two Glock 19s, extra ammo clips, door-buster explosive charges, flash-bang stun grenades, night vision, a Secret Service earpiece radio, climbing harness, carabiners, and other choice items.

Adam and Jeppesen walked outside onto the airport tarmac

to find a modified super quiet Sikorsky UH-60 Black Hawk helicopter. The machine's rotor blades were so silent, it had landed moments before without them hearing a thing.

That bode well for what they had in mind.

Adam climbed aboard, and the whisper-quiet 'copter rose to 10,000 feet and made a B-line for the Washington Monument.

At that moment, a Navy SEAL team made a giant, loud show of storming the monument at ground level. Knowing Sophia would have preset explosives, booby traps galore and who-knew-what else in place to prevent just such an assault, the SEALs were there to create a convincing diversion but had instructions to take every precaution not to get hurt.

The very top of the monument was a steeply sloping four-sided pyramid with two windows in each side. Sophia would have commanding views of all of Washington DC from those eight windows, but would have no way to look straight up. At least, that was Adam and Jeppesen's reasoning.

When the Black Hawk was directly above the monument, Adam stepped out into thin air. As the chopper silently descended straight down to 1,000 feet, a rope spooled out, lowering him another 500 feet. Oh-oh. A slight wind blew him off target by twenty yards. With his ear piece radio and mic he guided the pilot to bring him down onto the very peak of the steeply sloped top cap of the pyramid.

No-slip shoes or not, the pyramid's slope was way too steep. The 500-foot fall wouldn't be so bad, but the abrupt stop at the end didn't sound good. Adam had come prepared. He dropped a 10-foot-diameter lasso over the peak of the roof. A rope extending from the lasso to his climbing harness allowed him to belay out, body almost horizontal, and move around on the steep slope.

Letting out some rope, he inched himself down toward a window. The key was the element of surprise. He had explosives to blow the thing open, but it would be so much better if one was already open.

Belaying down, feet against the steep slope, making no sound, he eased down to where he could see the windows on the west side facing the Capitol Building. No luck. They were closed tight.

Moving with care, both for stealth and to keep from plunging to his death, he worked his way around the pyramid. The windows facing south were also closed.

He smiled to see in huge letters the Latin words *Laus Deo*, which in English essentially mean, "Glory Be to God," on the east side, the side facing the rising sun each morning. But here, too, the windows were shut tight.

Continuing his traverse—ha ha—he found both windows on the north side, the side facing the White House, wide open.

Perfect. Now he could toss in a stun grenade, swing out, drop in clean, and catch her completely by surprise. He'd need both hands to grip the rope and guide himself in. Then the moment he hit the deck inside, he'd whip out his pistols and finally capture this arch terrorist.

The flash-bang grenade dropped in and exploded beautifully. The swing went well. In an instant he was through the opening and balanced on the balls of his feet. But even before landing, he looked around and saw no one. Instead, he felt heavy netting drop from above and press in on all sides, pinning his arms. Completely enveloped and immobilized, struggle as he might, he was helpless.

Sophia stepped from behind a column. Apparently not much bothered by her wounded shoulder, she pushed him back onto a heavy bench, and duct-taped him in place, binding his neck to the bench back, his arms to his sides, and his ankles to the bench legs. Cutting small holes in the netting, she tore out his earpiece radio and removed his weapons. Outsmarted, humiliated, he'd dropped right into her trap.

Sophia wore a victorious, mocking, evil smile. "*As-Salaam-Alaikum*. Hi, Adam. How are you doing?"

"I'm good."

"I always liked your grace under pressure."

"I've got a few questions."

"Sure, you may as well go to your grave knowing what you were up against, what really happened, why you had no chance."

"What happened to George?"

"A very sweet boy. But he became suspicious. So, I caught him sitting, came up from behind, and snapped his neck."

Recoiling, Adam strained against his bindings, but to no avail. Somehow, he had to play for time, figure something out, come up with some way to stop this woman.

"How did you disable the White House drone shield?"

Sophia popped out her left eye, revealing a deep hole in her face. "Ha. Surprised? You'd be amazed the compact little remote-control bombs I can hide behind this fake eye."

"So, you're Cyclops?"

"I'm one-eyed, but my father, thank God, is the mastermind."

"Your father?"

"Abdul Kareem Aziz."

"So, you're not Sophia Katopodis?"

"I'm Fatima Sophia Aziz."

The idea that little Yoda-like Aziz could be Sophia's father defied belief, but so did the fanaticism that Aziz had instilled in his daughter.

"And Abdul Aziz is the mastermind? How'd that work?"

"Beautifully, praise Allah. What subordinate reveals his true nature to his boss? By keeping a low profile and pretending to be just an ordinary Believer, my father was able to move among our people and see each for who they truly are. To succeed—to win Allah's total support, as we obviously have—our people had to be pure, true, and devout. Besides, my brilliant father is truly humble and abhors the spotlight."

"I'll be blunt," Adam said, shaking his head inside the netting. "How could a well-educated, accomplished woman like you, with all you have going for you, embrace extreme fundamentalist Islamist terrorism? Don't you realize that—if you were to succeed—the freedoms bestowed by Western civilization would be swept away and the second-class status of women would become law?"

"I forgive you for that question. Your Western mind is blind to the true nature of the world. My father's love for me, my love for him, and our love for Allah surpasses all that. *Allahu Akbar.* Allah really, truly is great, and there is no other God but Allah."

"So why me? Why did you request me specifically?"

"Isn't it obvious? Your friendship with the president has been in the press for years. The goal, all along, was to be invited into the White House."

"So, you killed dozens of your people for that? How could you do that?"

"In case you didn't notice, most of them were deeply flawed. Masood Wahhab and the crew of *Saadet,* for example, were sinners and an affront to Allah. Roxanna was just too ambitious and full of herself. Of course, some were good, devout people who just had to be sacrificed for the greater good. As you people say, you can't cook an omelet without breaking some eggs."

"The cave explosion and the laptop erasure were your doing?"

"You're catching on. Maybe you're not so dumb."

"The prisoners off *Bora,* did they really threaten you?"

"Nope. Just had to kill 'em to keep 'em from blowing my cover."

"What about those assassination attempts on you?"

"Oh, that was Mossad," Fatima Sophia Aziz said, as she sat down on a bench facing Adam. "They were onto me. What a lucky break to have Jeppesen put out word I was dead. Otherwise the Israelis probably would have told you Americans to watch out for me. That was a close one. But Allah, as usual, was watching over me."

"How did you get bombs and drones here?"

"My brother, Ramzi, with our advance team, sailed into Chesapeake Bay and up the Potomac River a month ago."

"Your brother? Your dad?"

"I'm genuinely sorry you'll be dead and won't see it. Even if something were to happen to me, Ramzi and my father are unstoppable. Without doubt, we, or they, will decapitate the Great Satan."

"You have more nukes? More drones?"

"Of course, the roof of the Lincoln Memorial, being lower than the surrounding walls, makes an ideal staging area. Okay, I'll grant you your people thwarted the first grand attack. But we've got enough drones and bombs to demolish the Pentagon, Capitol Building, CIA, and FBI buildings, and still have bombs left over. It's going to be nuclear winter around here for a while."

"You realize you're insane. You've got to be stopped. You will be stopped."

"Adam, you don't realize your own importance. I have a feeling once you're dead, the wind, the will to resist, is going to go out of Tripnee and Jeppesen, the only people who have even the remotest idea what America is up against."

Sophia picked up an AK-47 lying on the bench beside her, and aimed it at Adam. "Well, enough of this. It's time to get on with it. I'm sorry you and I couldn't have met under other circumstances—with no Tripnee around. You're not bad for an infidel. But this is goodbye. *Allahu Akbar.*"

Swallowing, Adam blurted, "Would you grant a dying man one last wish? Would you do one of your twirls? I'll confess, I'm always mesmerized when you do that."

Sophia smiled in triumph. "Why not?" She put down her AK-47, brought her shapely form up from her bench, rose onto her tiptoes, and, in front of the window Adam had jumped through earlier, began a slow twirl.

At that precise moment, Sophia's head disappeared in a pink mist.

"What an absolutely terrific girlfriend," Adam said to the open window facing the White House.

AUTHOR'S NOTE

The events and characters described herein are fictional, while the places are real. Dream Voyager's route through the Greek Islands exactly matches the itinerary described in the author's short non-fiction sailing narrative "Sailing the Greek Islands: Dancing with Cyclops." The only difference being somewhat less bloodshed.

By the way, if you enjoyed this book, please post a review or two on Amazon, Good Reads, etc. Thank you!!!

—Bill McGinnis

ABOUT THE AUTHOR

 A California native with a Master's in English literature, William McGinnis wrote five non-fiction books about whitewater rafting and sailing—and now writes thriller novels—stories that captivate, delight, and inspire. Bill is well-known as the river-exploring founder of Whitewater Voyages. His passions include hiking, woodworking, staring into space, audiobooks, and exploring new paths to adventure, friendship, and growth. He lives in the San Francisco Bay Area. His author website is www.WilliamMcGinnis.com.

Books by William McGinnis:

Whitewater Rafting

The Class V Briefing

The Guide's Guide Augmented:
     Reflections on Guiding Professional River Trips

Sailing the Greek Islands: Dancing with Cyclops

Disaster on the Clearwater: Rafting Beyond the Limit

Whitewater: An Adam Weldon Thriller (#1)

Gold Bay: An Adam Weldon Thriller (#2)

Cyclops Conspiracy: An Adam Weldon Thriller (#3)

Coming Soon: *Slay the Dragon,* the fourth thriller in the Adam Weldon series.

China's relentless strategy of all-out unrestricted warfare—with the willing participation of bought-and-paid-for US elites—is bringing America to its knees. Can an ex-Navy SEAL, a tech-genius Chinese dissident, an Oakland cop, and a Silicon Valley billionaire save American democracy and put China on a better path? To find out, plunge headlong into this rousing, up beat, rip-roaring Adam Weldon thriller.

CPSIA information can be obtained
at www.ICGtesting.com
Printed in the USA
FSHW020459040821
83806FS